FEIGN

A CURVY GIRL ROMANTIC SUSPENSE

F-BOMB: CURVY VIGILANTES
BOOK 3

MARY E THOMPSON

Feign

F-BOMB: Curvy Vigilantes, book three

Ebook ISBN: 978-1-953879-32-5

Print ISBN: 978-1-953879-33-2

Audiobook ISBN: 978-1-953879-34-9

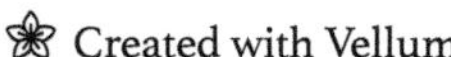 Created with Vellum

F-BOMB: CURVY VIGILANTES

Say hello to the Curvy Vigilantes, a group of plus-size women who protect their city. They have no training, but they don't need it. All they need is the desire to right wrongs and to protect the ones they love... and maybe some help from the men strong (and smart) enough to fall for these kick-ass curvy women.

F-BOMB: CURVY VIGILANTES

Forsaken (subscriber exclusive)

Fury

Framed

Feign

Fierce

Fatal

Fear

Flee

Fracture

Faith

SUBSCRIBE NOW AT MARYETHOMPSON.COM

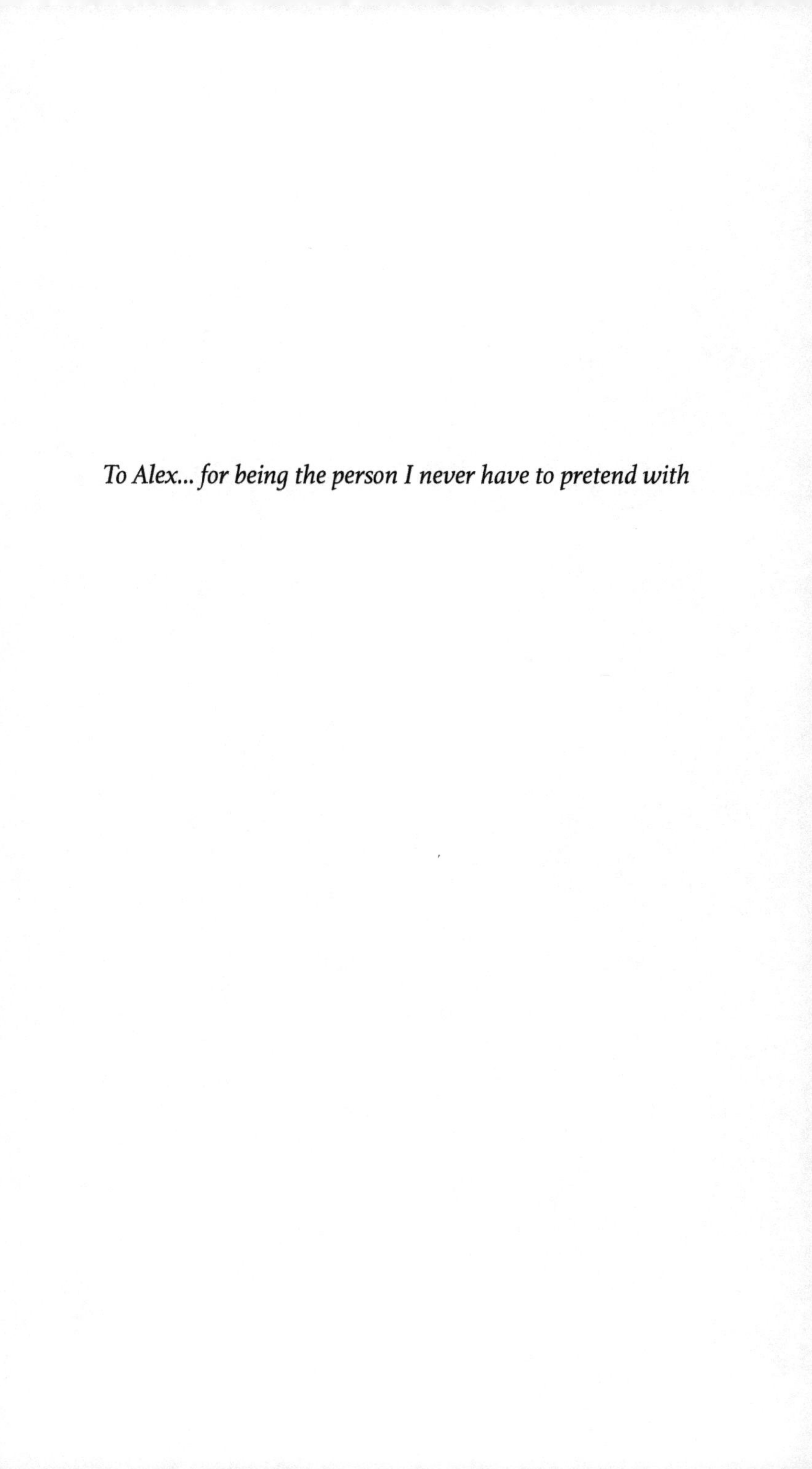

To Alex... for being the person I never have to pretend with

1

____

Karli Sloane knew the minute someone broke into her apartment. It was a feeling, like she was being watched, but deeper, like someone whispered she wasn't safe.

She was in her bedroom, taking off her jewelry after a quick trip out. Her best friend was coming over to share the dirty details of her first date with the guy she'd been lusting over forever. But whoever was in Karli's apartment was definitely not Jessica. Or Karli's roommate, Raina. It was someone else. Someone who was trying not to be heard.

Karli tiptoed to her bedroom door and peeked through the crack. She sucked in a silent breath. The woman could have been her twin. Especially at first glance. Same natural, shoulder-length dark curls. Same brown skin. Same full lips and wide nose. Even the woman's clothes were things Karli could have seen herself wearing.

For all her similarities, Karli had no idea who the woman was. She definitely would have recognized her if they'd met before, which brought back the question of why the hell she was in Karli's apartment and sneaking around like she was looking for something.

Stay or go? Fight or flee? Karli debated with herself for a few seconds as panic overwhelmed her and the need to run away consumed her. Then the woman walked into the kitchen, where Karli couldn't see her.

Adrenaline pumped in her veins, but not the good kind that made you fearless and fight. It was the bad kind that made Karli want to vomit and cry. The kind of adrenaline that would have her in a puddle if the woman discovered her.

Karli had to get the hell out of there. Now.

The fire escape outside her window was the only option. She didn't know why the woman was there, but Karli would get out and find a way to call the police.

She crept to the window and eased it open. Thankfully, she used it enough that it slid quietly. When she had just enough space to fit through, Karli squeezed her body out and closed the window so the woman wouldn't realize Karli had left.

She resisted the urge to race down the fire escape, knowing the metal stairs would be loud and draw attention. She was just out for a casual stroll down the fire escape. In the fall. No big deal. There wasn't any reason to be freaking out.

Besides the woman in her apartment.

Karli finally reached the ground and let out a heavy sigh of relief. She didn't want Jessica or Raina to arrive and encounter the woman, but her phone and purse were by the front door, and she had no way of letting her friends know what was going on. If she was lucky, she would catch them outside the building.

And if she wasn't, she'd catch the woman who broke into her apartment.

Karli leaned against the brick exterior near the front of

the building. She tried to blend in and look like she was waiting for someone. Her adrenaline was sky high, pulsing through her system and making her hyperaware of everything around her. The smell of exhaust when a truck went down the street. The blast of a horn when someone was cut off. The rumble of an engine, voices shouting, food from the burger place a block away.

It all yanked her attention, making it impossible to focus on one thing. She did her best, until she heard a siren.

It came closer, the rhythmic whoop echoing louder and louder until she saw the lights. Red and blue flashing, synchronized to the sounds. It was enough to make Karli take a step away from the door.

The cops ignored Karli and everyone else on the street and rushed inside. An ambulance pulled up a minute later. The paramedics didn't rush.

Karli watched the scene with a strange sense of detachment. Like she was witnessing it through a TV screen or someone else's eyes. She was numb, her fear making it hard for her to understand what was going on. Not that she knew what was going on. Someone else must have seen the woman and called the police.

"What happened?" someone asked a police officer as they walked out of the building.

"A woman was killed," the cop said. "We have to lockdown the building. Do you live here?"

The officer came toward the man who asked what happened. His hand rested on his hip, like he was getting ready to draw a weapon.

Karli backed away slowly so they didn't notice her. The officer and the man on the street talked. When Karli made it to the corner, she turned it and took off.

She didn't know where to go. Her purse with her phone

and wallet were inside the apartment. She had no way of reaching out to anyone. She didn't know what happened in the building and really didn't want to become a suspect for anything. Especially not for murder.

Niagara Falls wasn't the most walkable city, but it was okay. All she had to do was lie low for an hour or two and then she could go back home. She didn't have another option.

"ART THERAPIST, Karli Sloane, was murdered in her apartment earlier today. The police are looking for Jessica German for questioning. Ms. German was seen fleeing the apartment building where Ms. Sloane's body was found. I'm going to warn you, the picture you're going to see might be hard to handle."

Karli wanted to laugh when she heard the news report two hours after she left her apartment. For one thing, she was obviously not dead. For another, who in the world would ever think Jessica had anything to do with anyone's murder?

Karli rolled her eyes as she looked up at the screen. And saw her best friend covered in blood.

The news report clicked in her head. Jessica was wanted for questioning. The police thought Karli was dead. But someone was dead. And if Karli had to guess, it was the woman who'd been in her apartment. The one who looked like her. The one she fled because of.

She hated that she wondered, for a second, if Jessica could have had anything to do with it. She dismissed the idea as soon as she had it, but it lingered in the depth of her mind.

Karli wasn't safe. Whether Jessica had anything to do with killing that woman or not, Karli wasn't safe. She couldn't go back to her apartment. She couldn't go to Jessica. Raina could be in danger, but Karli didn't know how to contact her. Raina was smart, though. Raina would find a safe place. Karli just wished she knew of one.

Karli left the convenience store and walked toward the park a few blocks away. She'd always found the outdoors refreshing and invigorating. She had no intention of sleeping there, but for an hour, she could hang around.

She walked through the park and tried to figure out what was going on. Someone broke into her apartment, then was killed. She wasn't sure if she was more worried about the woman who broke in or the fact that someone killed her, but either way, Karli knew she wasn't safe. She was in danger. She had to find somewhere to hide.

After she left her apartment, Karli wandered for a few hours. She tried to go back, but there were still police cars sitting outside, so she left again, pretending she was just walking by. No one paid her any attention. She'd considered asking if she could get into her apartment, but it would have meant explaining where she lived and where she was when the woman was killed.

Now that Karli knew the police suspected it had been her, she was relieved she hadn't spoken to them. But she still needed somewhere to go. A place to sleep. Or at least shelter before the fall evening turned colder.

The evening air gave her a moment of clarity. If she could make her way to one of the big box stores that was open twenty-four-seven, she could stay inside and be safe. There were cameras in those stores, which meant someone would see if she was attacked. And she would be warm.

The walk there made Karli tense. She hadn't walked so

much in years. She was grateful she hadn't kicked off her shoes when she walked into her apartment. She didn't have money or a phone, but she had sneakers.

Inside the store, the bright lights and colorful displays were almost too much. But it was warm and safe and Karli knew it was her best option. She just had to pretend to be a customer and not give anyone any reason to be suspicious of her being there. Simple. Right?

CADE MURRAY HUNG up the phone and squeezed it tight. He wanted to throw it across the room, but he couldn't afford to buy another phone this month.

He knew something was wrong. His one and only client wasn't answering his calls. She hadn't since he told her he found someone who might know something about where her cousin was.

Why did he tell her?

Cade kicked himself for revealing the information. He was smarter than that. Well, he thought he was. Who the hell knew anymore. Cade also thought he was smarter than to get attached to a woman who would sleep with someone else, but he was wrong about that, too.

But this time, it was costing him what little future he had left as a private investigator. When Tonya Warren came to him and said her cousin had gone missing and she thought something had happened, Cade told her he wasn't interested. The last case he worked on blew up in his face in the most epic of ways, and he had become a laughingstock. He wasn't looking to take on a missing person case the police said wasn't worth investigating.

Tonya didn't show up without proof, though. She had

phone records and emails and financial documents that made it hard to believe anything other than her cousin was in serious trouble. And that one of the city's most notorious and invisible men was behind it.

Cade agreed to take the case, with a hefty retainer up front, and a contract for even more once he found Tonya's cousin, Edie. Tonya was happy to pay, but the second he shared information with her, she disappeared on him and stopped returning his calls.

Last time he trusted a woman.

It had been forty-eight hours since he'd spoken to Tonya. His research uncovered the name of a woman who used to be involved with Damon Street, the man Cade believed was responsible for Edie's disappearance. Tonya pushed him to reveal who the woman was. Cade wanted to do a little more digging into Raina London, confirm what he thought, and then talk to her. But Tonya was impatient. She said she just wanted to know the woman's name. Said she wondered if Edie had ever mentioned her.

Cade told her what he knew and what he suspected. It wasn't much, but anyone who used to be connected to a man like Damon Street and got out was someone Cade wanted to talk to.

Damon Street was notorious for being a ghost. The police had never arrested him. There were no pictures of the man. He was a legend, one Cade wasn't even sure was real. But if there was a chance, and Cade took him down, he would go from worst to first for private investigators in the area. No more mockery about not being able to see what was right in front of his face. He would be a legend himself.

But first he had to find out where the hell his client was.

Cade stuffed the file he had on Raina London into his bag with his computer and charger. It was going to be a long night, but before he could head home, he needed to find Tonya.

The motel Tonya was staying in was not the best place in the city. It was cheap, and it was clean, but it was old and small and had zero security. Which worked to Cade's advantage when he was able to go straight to Tonya's room instead of speaking to someone at the desk.

He parked near the staircase at the back of the parking lot, closest to Tonya's room. He glanced around before he took the stairs up. He knocked on her door, but there was no answer. He pressed his ear to the door. Nothing.

He glanced around again. He didn't see anyone around, so he dug out his lock-picking set. Tonya could be hurt. He justified his actions that way, even as he knew he could get into a lot of trouble for what he was doing.

A few seconds later, the cheap lock snicked open. Cade let himself in and closed the door behind him. He pocketed his kit and scanned the room quickly.

The bed was made, neat and tidy like it had been done by housekeeping and not a guest. The door to the bathroom was wide open. The light was off, but the shower curtain was thrown back, showing him how empty the bathroom was. There was a closed closet near the bathroom. Even though there was no way to surprise someone if they were hiding in it, Cade crept forward.

He yanked open the closet door and jumped back when the hangers swung at him. A small pile of clothes was on the floor in an open suitcase.

No Tonya.

Cade took a deep breath and stopped. He was trained to see what other people wouldn't notice. A dozen years in the Army, a degree in criminal justice, and close to seven years as a private investigator, Cade saw things differently.

Except when your girlfriend was fucking someone else.

Cade winced at the voice in his head. He sucked in a sharp breath and tried to push the thought away. Alanna was out of his life, but Tonya was not. And she was the one Cade needed to focus on.

The room looked like Tonya had just run out. Like she would be back at any minute. Her toothbrush was on the side of the sink, but it was dry. The shower had shampoo bottles in it, but again, it was dry. She had clothes in the dresser and a bottle of water on the nightstand. The entire place looked like nothing was out of the ordinary.

Which meant Tonya hadn't left town. She was still hanging around. So why wasn't she returning his calls?

Cade tried her phone again, but it went straight to voicemail like it had for two days. He looked around the room, wondering what he missed. He had to have missed something. But it all looked normal.

Which was never normal.

He decided to just wait for her. If Tonya ran out for something, she'd be back. Her purse was gone, but all her stuff was there. She'd be back. He knew it. He just had to wait.

CADE WOKE up to the sound of a car door slamming. An engine started. He looked around the motel room, but nothing had changed. Tonya wasn't in the bed. None of her stuff was missing or moved. She hadn't come back.

Could she have seen his car and decided to wait until he left? Or was something else going on?

Cade dragged himself out of the chair he made his bed overnight and wrote a quick note for Tonya to call him when she got back. He scribbled his number, even though she had it, just in case she lost her phone or something.

Then he left. He stopped by the welcome desk, but the man working there didn't know anything about Tonya. Had no idea the last time she'd been at the motel or even when she checked in. Said she left a card on file and had the room for two more weeks.

Cade went back to his office. He ran a trace on her phone, but as expected, it was off. Next, he got into her financial reports. Nothing had been used in two days.

"What the hell?"

She got breakfast the morning after they spoke at a diner near the motel. Then nothing. No more food, no gas, nothing. She could have used cash, but he found it unlikely since she'd been paying with credit up to that point.

Where could she be?

Cade turned on the TV in his office, listening to the newscaster drone on and on about crap he didn't care about. He was barely paying attention until he heard a report about a woman who was killed over the weekend.

He looked up at the screen and saw Tonya's picture.

No. It wasn't Tonya. She looked a lot like Tonya. And the newscaster called her Karli Sloane.

"Ms. Sloane was beloved by the kids she worked with. It seemed everyone adored her. To have her life cut short has shaken our community to the core."

Cade stared at her. She looked like Tonya. Remarkably. It was strange. There were differences between them if you looked closely enough, but at a glance, they could have been sisters.

"Ms. Sloane's funeral will be tomorrow at noon. All the information is on our website."

Cade didn't know why he wanted to go to the woman's

funeral, but he knew he had to. If for no other reason than to distract himself from his own missing client.

Tonya had to be out there somewhere. And if a woman who looked just like her was killed, maybe she found Raina London, and maybe Raina London was still connected to Damon Street.

Cade had to find Tonya. Now.

2

———

CADE FOUND A SEAT AT THE BACK OF THE CHURCH FOR THE funeral. It was a huge celebration of life for a woman who touched many in the community. Some of her patients spoke about how beloved she was. A friend talked about how amazing Karli had been. Her brother shared how proud he was of his sister and how hard she'd always worked.

All of it made Cade wish he'd met the woman. She was clearly someone who gave of herself. Someone who was generous and kind and good.

After seeing the news report about her, Cade looked into Karli Sloane. She shared the same address as Raina London, which piqued his curiosity even more than her similarities to Tonya. Even though Cade gave Raina's name and address to Tonya, the fact that Karli lived there, too, made Cade pause and wonder about the woman. About both of them.

He wasn't sure what he thought he'd find at the funeral, but he walked outside feeling like he didn't find it. The afternoon was bright and sunny and beautiful. A light rain began to fall as he made his way toward his car. Cade hurried before it got worse, and then he saw her.

Tonya.

She was on the other side of the parking lot, walking away. But it was her. He rushed to catch up to her, but she was too far away.

"Tonya!" he called out.

Someone glared at him as he rushed past them, clearly too loud for a funeral. Cade waved in apology and kept going.

"Tonya!"

She didn't stop. She didn't even slow down. It was like she hadn't heard him at all.

What the hell?

He finally made it to where she was, but she was gone. Lost in the crowd of mourners walking toward the graveyard.

Cade abandoned his decision to leave right after the funeral and joined the others heading to the burial site. He hung back, looking for Tonya in the crowd. He didn't know how Tonya knew Karli Sloane, or if she even did, but if Tonya was there, there was a reason. He just had to find out what it was.

Karli's family sat together, but every time the funeral director asked a question, they looked at another woman, a white woman Cade didn't know. She was the one calling the shots.

Cade pulled out his phone and took a picture of her without anyone noticing. He didn't know her connection, but there was one. And if she had a connection to Karli, she might have a connection to Raina or Damon or Tonya's cousin.

Cade scanned the guests once more. He didn't see Raina

London, which was odd since they'd been roommates. He didn't know anyone else in Karli's life, but he'd expected to see Raina. Most of the others were wiping their eyes and focused on the coffin as it was carried toward the hole in the ground where the woman inside would rest for eternity.

Funerals were an odd thing for Cade. The finality of it. He could still remember his grandmother's funeral when he was nine. She was the only person in his life who acted like he mattered when he was a child. His parents were wholly focused on Cade's older brother, Jackson, Jr., and everything JJ did. Cade was an afterthought at best, but usually not even that.

Except with his grandmother. Her entire face would light up when Cade walked into a room. She always looked for him. He was her favorite person in the entire world. She said he reminded her of her late-husband, the grandfather Cade never met. She told Cade stories about him and made him feel like he could do anything. He was the reason Cade joined the Army. His grandfather had done the same, and the stories his grandmother told him made him want to be a hero, too.

When she got sick, Cade was the only one who could make her smile. And when it was the end, she wanted him there with her. He missed three days of school to be by her side for her last days.

Her death rocked his world. Everything changed overnight for Cade. Instead of having someone who adored him, he was alone. That was what death did. It stole people. It left the ones behind feeling like a piece was missing.

And watching as Karli's family and friends mourned her was like losing his grandmother all over again. He couldn't explain it, but after researching her for an entire day, he felt like he knew Karli Sloane. The woman she was and the one she would have been.

Cade was so busy watching the coffin that he almost didn't notice Tonya standing on the far side of the graveyard, away from the guests. Cade couldn't call out to her in the middle of the ceremony, but he had to talk to her. Find out where she'd been for two days and if she went to Raina's apartment like he assumed.

Maybe also find out why another woman was dead.

He moved toward the back of the crowd, keeping his gaze on Tonya. When he reached the edge of the gatherers, he moved around the group and started toward her. He glanced back when a bell sounded. The coffin started to sink. Slowly.

Cade closed his eyes and said a prayer for the woman in the coffin. That she would find peace.

Then he turned back to Tonya. She was gone. Again.

"Dammit," he hissed, earning a glare from the people near him.

He pressed his lips up into an apologetic smile and moved away from the group. He had a camera in his SUV. Tonya couldn't have gotten far. Maybe she was still there. And maybe he could find her.

The lot was quiet when he got back to it. His SUV wasn't blocked in, but he wasn't as ready to leave as he'd been after the service.

Cade grabbed his camera from the front floorboard and adjusted the focus. He took pictures of the entire crowd around the graveyard. From the family and friends to patients and parents. He didn't see Tonya, but he kept taking pictures.

The crowd finally started to disburse. He sat in his vehicle, but he couldn't take pictures without someone noticing. He watched, waiting for Tonya to reappear.

One by one, the vehicles in the lot pulled out. People hugged and cried and shared words, but they all left. When Cade was the only one left, he knew it was time to go.

He turned toward his apartment and remembered he needed dinner for the night. Groaning since the store was the other way, he decided to run into the big box store. If he was lucky, it would be quiet since it was only three o'clock.

Cade grabbed a basket and headed for the frozen foods aisle. He stared at the choices, none of them overly appealing. He had to eat something, though. He grabbed five options and tossed them into his cart. He went to the back of the store and picked up a six-pack of local beer. He was on his way up front when he saw the hair again.

Tonya. What the hell was she doing there?

He followed her down an aisle, but she turned at the other end before he could say something to her. He rolled his eyes at himself and kept going, spotting her again in the chips aisle.

She glanced up when he turned the corner, but she immediately looked away. She busied herself looking at chips.

There was something about the way she was standing there that tugged at him. She was familiar, but not. He thought she was Tonya, but for the brief moment she met his gaze, there was no recognition in hers. Even if Tonya had been avoiding him, she would have reacted to seeing him.

Which meant the woman in front of him wasn't Tonya.

And unless she had a twin, Cade had a sinking feeling he knew exactly who she was.

He walked closer to her, pretending he was just looking for chips. He grabbed a bag from close to where she was standing, knowing she would look up at him if he moved into her personal space.

He flashed her a smile. "Sorry. These are my favorites."

She smiled back and nodded, moving a few feet away.

He pulled out his phone and swiped to open the camera app. "What else is on my list?" It was a crappy ploy, but if he was lucky... Yes!

She looked up, and he snapped a picture of her face.

"Apples. Love fresh apples in the fall. My favorite time of year."

She smiled again and nodded.

Point taken, and mission accomplished.

"Have a nice night," Cade said as he turned.

She didn't reply, but she didn't have to. Cade got what he needed. Confirmation she was not Tonya, and a picture to prove what he already knew.

Karli Sloane was alive.

KARLI WATCHED the man retreat and finally let out the breath she'd been holding. She wasn't usually the woman men noticed or spoke to in the grocery store. With her thick legs and wide hips, she was ignored more than anything else. Unless she was blocking an aisle. Then she was granted a dirty look.

The man who walked away was just being friendly. She knew people who would talk to anyone and figured he had to be one of those people. That's the only reason he said anything to her.

She hadn't noticed him before he spoke and barely saw him after. Her head was spinning. She'd actually attended her own funeral. People always said they wondered what others would say about them, and Karli knew the answer. But it wasn't real.

Her parents and brothers came, which she appreciated. There was a part of her that wondered if they'd even bother, but obviously Stacey had contacted them. Karli's cousin, Lorelei, was there, too. They'd been close once, but it had been a while since Karli had spoken to her. Stacey was the one calling the shots and had obviously been the one to make all the arrangements. Karli appreciated it, more than Stacey would ever know. Raina wasn't there, and neither was Jessica. Karli wasn't surprised, but she wanted to see her friends. To know they were safe.

Karli hated seeing all her patients there. To know they all thought she was gone. She adored each of them and almost lost it when they started talking about how great she was. For all the times over the last few days she'd felt like crap for running instead of facing the woman in her apartment, none were as bad as knowing her patients were suffering.

But the more Karli thought about it, the more she knew she had no choice but to stay hidden.

Karli continued to stare at the chips as her stomach rumbled loudly. She hoped no one heard. There were times it was tempting to grab something off the shelves and eat it in the store, but Karli couldn't handle the idea of stealing.

When she was sure the man who'd spoken to her was gone, she moved away from the chips. She went to the baby section and touched all the soft, pretty things. Then she went to office supplies. After walking around for an hour, she decided to get more fresh air before finding her hiding place for the night.

Karli was sick of finding food and starving. She was sick

of sleeping in a chair. She was sick of walking hours a day. She wanted a shower and a bed and a good meal.

But more than all of that, she wanted to stay alive. So she kept going. Walking and scavenging and sleeping wherever she could.

KARLI FINALLY HAD ENOUGH after almost a week of hiding in plain sight. She ended up in a long line of fans heading toward the high school on Friday night. She had no idea what was going on, but there was a crowd and they were all distracted.

The school was open for people to use the bathroom. Karli went in and found herself in a locker room instead of just a regular bathroom. She nearly cried when she saw the open lockers with clothes and food inside.

Glancing around to make sure no one else was there, Karli grabbed a granola bar from one locker. She snagged a bottle of pop from another. A third came up with an apple. An empty string bag with the high school logo on it was sitting on the end of a bench. Then she found clothes. A sweatshirt, pants, even a t-shirt.

Not all of it was exactly her size, but it was close enough.

She kept moving through the locker room and found the showers. It was an open space, but it was separated from the rest of the locker room. She felt like she'd hit the jackpot.

Without thinking about what she was doing, Karli turned on the shower. She had to be quick, but she didn't care. It was better than trying to clean herself in the bathroom at the big box store and always feeling like she wasn't clean enough.

After her shower, she dressed in the borrowed clothes.

She felt guilty taking things from students, but her right-eousness was slipping the longer she was on her own, scared, hungry, and dirty.

One day, she'd repay all the people who unknowingly helped her.

She checked to make sure the locker room was still empty, then left. She made it outside and hoped the crowd was still lingering so she could disappear into it again.

Thankfully, there was a small group just outside the door. She walked past them, pumping her fist when they cheered for the school she'd just adorned herself as a fan of.

Karli pulled her hood up and glanced around. It was risky sneaking into the high school for a shower, but it had been too long since she had one. She needed to feel clean. Or cleaner.

She turned toward the baseball field and ducked her head, hoping to blend into the crowd and disappear before anyone recognized her. The sweatshirt she swiped from the locker room was big enough that she could wear her pilfered backpack underneath and hide that she was carrying her dirty clothes and not much else with her.

"Good game, huh?" a guy asked her.

Karli nodded. "Definitely."

"Think they can hold on to the lead?"

"I hope so." Karli flashed the guy a smile, avoiding his gaze. She hoped that was the right answer. She didn't know what the score was or who was winning, but she was going to play along.

"Me, too. My son's the right fielder. He said the team really wants to win this game for Coach Tom. They want to make it to the playoffs for his last season."

"That's nice of them," Karli said. She kept pace with the guy. In another lifetime, she might have let herself think he was cute. Short dark hair, a nice smile, and the kind of eyes a woman could get lost in. If she wasn't already lost. Or trying to be.

"Yeah. He's been a great coach. Definitely goes above and beyond for these kids. Do you have a kid who's playing?"

Karli shook her head. "No. I'm here with a friend."

"Oh, yeah? Does your friend have a kid on the team? Jake has all the kids over sometimes. I probably know him."

Karli searched her mind for the little she knew about baseball. "Um, yeah. He's the pitcher. One of them."

"Roger? Nick? Antonio? Jerome?"

"Yeah, Jerome."

The guy nodded and kept walking with her.

"So, I should go find my friend. Enjoy the rest of the game."

"You, too, Karli."

Karli stopped in the middle of the sidewalk. "What? Um, what did you call me?"

"Karli. Isn't that your name? Karli Sloane?" He turned and looked at her, crossing his arms over his wide chest. He raised one eyebrow.

"How... I mean, no. You must have me confused with someone else."

"Actually, no, I don't. Because you're Karli Sloane." He took a step closer to her.

"Isn't that the woman who was found dead in her apartment a while ago? Her friend killed her, right?" Karli tried to play off the accusation even as her entire body flushed hot and broke into a sweat.

"Except her friend didn't kill her. But you already know that, Karli. Since, you know, you're not dead and Jessica didn't kill anyone."

"Who are you?"

He smirked, the edge of his lips turning up. He knew he caught her. They both did.

Every instinct in her said to run, but there was something about the look in his eyes that said he was smirking because he figured it out, not because he was going to turn her in.

"What do you want?" Karli asked.

"Answers."

"What kind of answers?"

"The kind I think you can help me get. Starting with who actually killed the woman in your apartment."

"I don't know. I don't even know who she was."

"Her name was Tonya Warren. She hired me to find her cousin. She thought you knew something. Or the woman who was staying with you did."

"Raina?"

The man nodded.

"Wait a minute. How did you find me? How did you know who I was? How do you know all of this?"

"Because I've been following you, Karli. And you're the only one who can help me. Will you? Please?"

Karli looked at him. He was a stranger. He'd been following her. He hadn't turned her in, or outed her. He wanted to help her. If they worked together, she could get her life back.

But first, she had to trust him.

3

Cade watched as the war waged in Karli's brown eyes. He shouldn't be thinking about how beautiful she was, but it was impossible when he was standing so close to her and had a good look at her for the first time. Her curves were sensuous and tempting. The way she chewed on her bottom lip made him want to have a taste. And the unease in her gaze... that made him want to take her back to his apartment and make sure she knew she was safe.

But first, she had to agree to help him. Because Tonya was dead because of him. And he was going to find out not only who killed her but why. Whether Karli wanted to help him or not.

"How do I know this isn't a trap?"

Cade shook his head and started walking toward the parking lot past the football field. "You don't. But my name is Cade Murray. I'm a private investigator. I was working with Tonya for a few weeks. The last time I spoke to her, I mentioned I'd found your roommate, Raina. Tonya believed her cousin was taken as part of some criminal organization. Either wrong place, wrong time, or because Edie got involved in something way over her head. The only thing Tonya cared about was finding her cousin, and we believed Damon Street would know something."

"Raina's ex?" Karli blurted.

Cade nodded.

"I knew he was bad news, but part of a criminal organization?"

"What I really need is to speak to Raina. Do you know how I can get in touch with her?"

Karli chewed on the inside of her cheek and shook her head. Her gaze drifted away. She was hiding something.

"She's clearly not staying at your apartment any longer. Where would she have gone?"

"I don't know. I haven't been in touch with anyone. Since, you know, they all think I'm dead."

"Raina wasn't at your funeral. Why?"

"How do you know that?" Karli drew back half a step.

"I told you, I've been following you. I saw the report on the news and how similar you and Tonya look and decided to go to your funeral. When I looked into you and found out you lived with Raina, I knew there was a connection between you, Raina, and Tonya. What I'm not sure is what the connection is."

"All I know is Tonya broke into my apartment. She was sneaking around my home. I got the hell out of there. I didn't know who she was or why she was there. If she'd knocked on the door and asked about Damon, I'm sure Raina would have been happy to share everything she knew. She left him. She nearly killed her. She's been staying with me because he was abusive and horrible and she'd be dead if he found her."

"Tonya is dead," Cade snarled. "She is dead. And if you or your friend know something, you need to come forward and tell the police. Something like the woman in your grave isn't you."

A loud cheer echoed from the nearby football field. The band started to play. Smiling fans streamed out of the stands and flowed toward the parking lot. Cade knew Karli had no idea what was going on when he started talking to her about baseball. It wasn't even baseball season, which he was sure she didn't know. But it meant he could get her talking if he played along. And then he could find out more about what really happened.

He wasn't sure if he believed Karli's story. If she really did leave before Tonya was killed, why wouldn't she go to the police?

"Whoever killed your friend is still out there."

"You mean Jessica?" Cade asked.

"Jessica didn't do it," Karli snapped.

Finally, some emotion. Cade hoped to pull some out of her. To see the streak that could have led to her attacking Tonya. "If she didn't, then who?"

"I don't know. I told you, I left. There was a stranger in my apartment, sneaking around. I wasn't going to walk out and ask what she was doing there. I had no way of knowing if she was dangerous or what she wanted. I was scared."

"So you ran?"

"Yes," Karli said. She glanced around as the crowd surrounded them.

"I need to find out what happened to her," Cade said.

Karli nodded. "I understand. But Jessica didn't do it. She's a good person. She would never have hurt anyone."

"What about you, Karli? Are you a good person?"

Karli's gasp was audible above the noise of the crowd around them. Her eyes widened. She took a step away from him, bumping into someone.

"Excuse me," she said.

"No worries! Great game, wasn't it?"

"Excellent," Karli told the man.

"Karli," Cade said.

He watched as she slipped past the man she bumped into. He made a move to get to her, but she ducked behind someone else. She weaved through the thick crowd and disappeared in five seconds.

Cade wanted to scream, but he knew that wouldn't help. He stopped in the middle of the crowd, earning glares and a few choice words from the people filing around him toward their vehicles.

"Dammit!" he hissed under his breath.

He knew she was going to try to get away from him, but he thought he'd be able to see it coming and stop her. She was the last person to see Tonya alive, except for possibly her killer. If Karli wasn't the one who killed Tonya, she was likely the killer's target.

She was the key. The key to finding Tonya's killer and the key to finding Raina and Tonya's cousin, Edie. It didn't matter than Tonya was dead, Cade was going to do every-thing he could to find her cousin and bring her back.

But first he had to find Karli Sloane. Again.

KARLI DIDN'T LOOK BACK as she rushed away from Cade. At first, he seemed like someone she could trust. Honest and kind and helpful. But the more they talked, the more it sounded like he wanted to bring her in for murder instead of help her figure out what actually happened in her apart-ment after she left.

Of course, he clearly didn't believe her about leaving

before anything happened to Tonya. That was something Karli didn't see coming. He thought she was a killer.

When she made it to the road at the end of the parking lot, she weaved in and out of the other people walking toward their vehicles. She didn't know what Cade drove, but there was no doubt he would be out looking for her. She had to find somewhere to hide until he was gone.

Karli thought, for the millionth time, about calling Jessica's boss to find out if her boyfriend and his team could help her. Jessica worked for a clothing designer, but Taylor, her boss, was dating a former SEAL who kept people safe. Dex and his team would get to the bottom of everything. The only issue was Karli had never met Taylor or Dex or any of them. She could call and end up trusting the wrong person and regretting it.

She kept walking as the crowd thinned and people got into their vehicles to head home. She knew walking down the street was a bad idea, so Karli turned into a small neighborhood and acted like she knew where she was going. After a few minutes, she came to a park with a playground and no one around.

There was a small building on the far side of the playground. It could be a good place to hide for the night, or it could be the worst idea ever, but Karli didn't see another option. If she stayed out in the open, someone would report her or catch her. And if she walked too long, Cade would find her.

She made her way to the building and tested the door. It gave after a few tugs, letting her into the storage room. There was a small bathroom at the back of the room. It was cramped and smelled slightly of mold, but it was better than a jail cell. Or a grave.

Karli made herself at home for the night. Every whisper

of the wind outside made her jump. When the swings creaked in the breeze, she froze. But when the sun finally came up, she let out a sigh of relief.

If Cade was following her, Karli needed to do something different. Going back to the same places she'd been going was out of the question. She needed to change her routine. And maybe find out a few things about Cade Murray, and if he really was who he said he was.

TEN MORE DAYS went by for Karli, hiding in a different place every day. She'd used the library to research Cade and found out he was who he claimed to be. But if he was trying to get her, or Jessica, arrested, or if he was after Raina, she needed to be careful.

Karli was in a convenience store, using cash she swiped from a gas station the week before. Her cheeks burned as she walked up to the register and paid for her breakfast burrito with stolen money. She felt as though the clerk would know she was a thief. God, she hated it. Her stomach churned and guilt swelled inside her. Even though she knew she had no other choice, she hated who she'd become in just a few weeks.

"Jessica German, the woman accused of killing local art therapist, Karli Sloane, was brought into the police station last night."

Karli froze at the report playing loudly behind the desk. The clerk's gaze stayed on his phone as the reporter continued.

"Another man was brought in with her, a man police are now saying was the lead suspect. Ms. German had no connection to the man, and she was released from police custody after being questioned last night. The suspect, Silver James, died before he was police were able to question him. His death is currently under investigation."

"Damn," the clerk said, reaching for Karli's burrito to ring it up. "I thought for sure she did it."

Karli ducked her head and made a sound of agreement. She didn't want to get into a discussion with the guy.

"Two-sixty-seven."

She handed over three dollars and waited, her gut twisting in fear and impatience, while he counted out her change.

"Need a receipt."

"Nope," Karli said. "Have a good day."

He ignored her and went back to his phone as the reporter moved on to another story.

All Karli could think was she had to find Jessica. She had to find out what happened. And make sure her friend was okay.

Karli ate her breakfast burrito and walked the streets toward the residential part of the city. Jessica lived in a condo, but Karli knew she wouldn't go there. If she had to guess, Jessica would end up with Stacey. Stacey worked at Shelter in the Storm, a shelter that took in women and children who needed a safe place to stay. It was where Raina went after Damon almost killed her, and Karli assumed where Raina was again.

But it was early, and Stacey might still be home. That was where Karli was headed.

When she finally made it to Stacey's neighborhood, she breathed a sigh of relief. She still needed to find Stacey's house. They hadn't known each other long or well, but Jessica told Karli where Stacey lived. Karli just hoped her memory was good enough to get her to the right house.

She peeked in the windows of the first house she thought might be Stacey and Wray's, but the family at the kitchen table wasn't familiar. Karli backed away before she was seen and kept moving. The second house was dark, but a vehicle in the driveway had a bumper sticker for the local high school and Stacey's boys were too young.

Karli found a third house that could have fit the description Jessica shared. A truck in the driveway had a fire department sticker on the back window. A car sat next to it with a third vehicle behind that one.

Karli saw a video doorbell from the road and knew she had to avoid it if she was going to check that it was the right house.

A light came on upstairs. She watched for movement, smiling when the curtains were pulled back and revealed a man at the window. Wray.

Bingo.

Karli still didn't want anyone to see her, so she crept up to the door and avoided the camera as long as she could. She looked through the sidelight but couldn't see anyone else inside. There was a light on toward the back of the house, but that was it.

Karli rang the bell and waited. A few seconds later, the door opened. A shocked Stacey gasped. "Oh, my God. How are you here?"

Before Karli could answer, Stacey pulled her in for a tight hug.

"I didn't know what to do. I knew someone was after me, but until I saw the news this morning, I didn't know where to go or what to do."

"Come back here. Now. Jessica, Raina, and Frannie are here."

"I know," Karli said, following Stacey into the house. "That's why I came."

"Karli?" Jessica and Raina said at the same time.

Karli stepped into the kitchen and almost cried when she saw her friends.

"How are you here?" Frannie asked. "We thought you were dead."

"So did whoever thought they killed me. That's why I've been hiding."

"He's dead. Jessica found him. Damon was behind it all."

"I know. What I don't know is who it was that they killed. But she wasn't supposed to be there. She broke in."

"What?" Jessica asked.

"You saw her?" Raina asked.

Karli nodded. "I saw her. And she looked just like me. I have no idea who she was or why she was in my apartment, but I need to find out."

Frannie and Stacey exchanged a look. Stacey went to a cabinet on the far side of the kitchen. She pulled out a bottle of wine and carried it back to the table. She twisted off the top and took a swig straight from the bottle, then handed it to Karli.

Karli smiled and nodded, then took a drink. She passed it on to Raina, then Jessica, then Frannie.

When Stacey got the empty bottle back, she gestured to the table. Karli took the seat she'd vacated and met the gazes of four women she wasn't sure she'd ever see again.

"Start at the beginning and tell us everything," Frannie said.

Karli did. She told them about the woman breaking in and fleeing as soon as possible. About waiting outside the building to try to find Jessica and Raina, and apologized for not stopping Jessica before she went in. Karli told them about hiding once she realized the woman was dead and that whoever killed her was likely looking for Karli. And then she told them about Cade Murray and the story he told her.

"He knows you're alive?" Frannie asked.

Karli nodded. "He called me by name. He definitely knew who I was. He said I looked just like the woman he was working for."

"Tonya Warren," Raina said.

Karli nodded again. "That's what he said her name was, but I don't know if any of it is true."

"And all of this has to do with Damon. Which means I brought this to your doorstep. I'm the reason that woman is dead, and the reason you were almost killed," Raina said. Her voice was shaky and broke on the last word. Tears streamed down her cheeks as she squeezed her eyes shut.

"No, you are not," Frannie said firmly. "That monster of an ex is responsible for all of this. It is not your fault. His actions are his own. We've talked about this."

Raina nodded and drew a shaky breath. She sat up straighter and lifted her gaze to Karli's. "I'm sorry for what he did. And I'm sorry I ever put you in danger."

"You have nothing to apologize for. You didn't know who he was when you met. You thought he was a decent guy. If you'd known, you never would have gotten involved with him. Now that you know, you're trying to live your life. You're trying to get free of him. That's not a bad thing. You're strong and brave and you can't ever stop fighting." Karli reached across the table to squeeze Raina's hand.

"I won't. I know he'll kill me if I ever go back to him. Or if he finds me."

"We're not going to let that happen," Frannie assured Raina.

"So, why was this Tonya woman at your apartment?" Jessica asked.

"She was looking for information about her cousin. Cade said he found your name, Raina, and somehow knew you used to be involved with Damon. He thinks Damon is connected to the cousin's disappearance. Tonya came to our place to, I don't know, talk to you or confront you or see what she could find. She wanted to find her cousin. If what Cade said is true."

"I'll be right back," Frannie said, lifting her phone as she walked away.

"The more I find out about Damon, the worse of a human I realize he is. How did I let myself fall for him?" Raina asked.

"You didn't choose to. He showed you who he wanted you to see. You're a good person, and you would have left him sooner if you knew who he really was." Jessica reached over and grasped Raina's hand.

"I know, but—"

"No," Stacey said. "He doesn't get to have power over you. You fell for someone else. You don't get to second guess that. There was no way for you to know who he was. All we have to do now is move forward and take him down."

"Do we really think that's possible?" Karli asked.

"No," Raina said.

"Yes," Jessica and Stacey said together.

"He's evil. And he's worse than any of us knew. I know Oscar is the one who killed Holly, but I believe Damon, or someone in his organization, is the one who killed Oscar. His suicide was too convenient. Just like Silver's death last night at the police station." Stacey met Jessica's gaze.

Jessica shivered.

"What happened? The news said he died in police custody and it's under investigation," Karli said.

Jessica laughed mirthlessly. "They were coming to let me go. They knew it was Silver who killed... Tonya, I guess, but anyway. Marcus had just released me and Braden was going to take me home—"

"Braden?" Karli barked. A smile lifted her lips for the first time in weeks.

Jessica returned her grin. "Yeah. Long story, but yeah." Jessica's cheeks darkened and a secret smile settled on her face. "Anyway, we were about to leave and another cop was going to question Silver. They were doing CPR when we walked up, and they pronounced him dead. One of the cops gave him a bottle of water, and Marcus said it was likely laced with something."

"Seriously?" Karli asked.

Jessica nodded. "Someone inside the police station silenced him. Which means there's a cop who's working for Damon, too."

"Holy shit," Karli breathed.

Jessica nodded. "We're fighting a ghost."

Karli grinned. "Maybe it's good I'm a ghost, too."

4

———

"Good news," Frannie said, walking back into the kitchen. "Cade Murray is legit. And the picture on his website is actually him."

"He is?" Karli asked. "How do you know?"

"I called Marcus. He knows him. Checked the site. Said he's a PI."

"Is he good?"

"Marcus didn't say that. It sounds like he had a case go sideways about a year ago, but Marcus didn't tell me what it was about. But it sounds like this Tonya caught the attention of the department, too. She's been asking questions and bugging them about her cousin, Edie Warren. Marcus said they looked into her disappearance, but there were no signs of foul play, so there was nothing they could do. It's an open case, but a cold case with no evidence that could explain what happened to her."

"When did she disappear?" Karli asked.

"In the spring," Frannie said.

"And no one's seen or heard from her?" Jessica asked.

"Nope," Frannie answered.

"That's suspicious," Raina said.

"Do you recognize her name?" Karli asked Raina. "Edie Warren."

Raina shook her head. "I'd already left him by then, but Damon didn't talk about work with me. When we started dating, he told me he was in shipping. Said it was boring work moving items around. He brushed off any questions I ever had as nothing I'd be interested in and would ask about me. He was smart. He got me talking about myself and my interests and then he would insert himself into whatever I was doing. He seemed like a doting boyfriend, until I moved in with him. Then I started to see his dark side. He would have secret phone calls and meetings and would never let me out of the bedroom when someone came over. He would actually lock me in, and if I didn't make noise…"

Karli stared at her friend, afraid of what she was going to say.

Stacey put an encouraging hand on Raina's shoulder and nodded.

Raina sucked in a breath. "If I behaved, he would reward me with orgasms. If I didn't behave and whoever he was talking to heard me, even something like flushing the toilet, he would punish me. Force himself on me and get angry if I tried to come."

"I'm so sorry," Karli told her. Bile lifted in her throat imagining Raina having to go through that. Raina was a light, a brightness the world needed, and to have someone take that away was painful to even think about.

"You're safe now," Frannie said.

"Thanks to all of you. But there's a woman who's dead, and she has a cousin who's missing. Are we really going to let him get away with it?" Raina asked.

One by one, they shook their heads.

"He sent someone to kill me," Karli said. "He framed Jessica for it. There's no telling how many others he's killed or will kill. We have to stop him."

"How are we going to do that?" Jessica asked.

"All of you are going to go on like nothing happened. I'm the ghost. I can get answers," Karli said.

"How?" Raina asked.

"I'm going to reach out to Cade Murray. He knows more than we do."

"Where are you staying?" Stacey asked.

"I don't know," Karli admitted. "I knew my apartment wasn't safe."

"No, definitely not," Frannie said. "The shelter is full right now, but—"

"I wouldn't stay there. I'm guessing that's where you are, Raina."

Raina nodded at Karli.

"There's only one reason Damon would come after me. He's trying to get to you. I'm not going to stay where you are and give him a beacon. He might know you're there, but I'm not going to make it even more obvious." Karli looked at Jessica.

"Braden asked me to stay with him. The police tore my place apart and I'm just not ready to be alone. I can ask—"

"Nope," Karli said. "I'll make it part of my agreement with Cade. He has to find a place for me to stay and guarantee my safety if he wants my help."

"What if he can't?" Stacey asked.

"Then I'll figure something else out, but I'm not putting any of you in danger. I stayed away this long because I didn't want to risk anyone else getting hurt, but I knew I had to talk to you. Especially when I heard the news."

The others nodded.

The front door opened, then closed. Heavy footsteps led straight toward them. Karli's entire body froze, fear taking over her.

Braden Wright walked into the kitchen and stopped dead. "What... How... Holy fuck. You're alive?"

Jessica stood and took the bags from him, handing them to Stacey and Raina. She cupped his jaw and brought his gaze to hers. "She's alive."

"Holy shit," Braden breathed. He leaned down and kissed Jessica hard on the mouth, then pulled back with a wide grin and moved toward Karli. He lifted her out of her chair and wrapped her in his big arms. "I'm so happy you're alive."

"Um, thanks," Karli said.

Braden pulled back and ran a hand through his hair. "Sorry. I know we've met like twice, but Jessica's been talking about how amazing you are for weeks and I hated that she'd lost such a wonderful person in her life. But you're alive. Holy fuck, you're alive. Wait, how are you alive?"

The women all laughed. Jessica grabbed his hand and pushed him into the seat she was in, then sat on his lap. They filled him in, then repeated all the information when Wray came downstairs and realized a dead woman was in his kitchen.

Karli was starting to feel normal again. Like she could have a life. But when everyone made moves to leave, she knew her life wasn't normal yet.

"Do you want a ride somewhere?" Jessica asked.

"I'll be okay," Karli told her.

"We will take you anywhere. Where are you staying?" Braden asked. His arm was around Jessica's shoulders. They looked happy. In love. Like they'd been together forever instead of just had their first date a few weeks earlier.

Karli knew Jessica would eventually tell her the whole story, but for the moment, Karli was happy to see her friend safe and smiling.

"Do you know where Cade Murray's office is?" Jessica asked.

Karli shook her head. "I was thinking of calling him tomorrow."

"Where are you staying tonight?" Braden asked.

"I don't know yet."

"Come home with us," Braden said.

"No. You two have been through hell. You need time together. I'm not going to get in the middle of that," Karli insisted.

"We have the rest of our lives," Braden said. He pulled Jessica closer and kissed her lips gently, his gaze locking on hers. "For today, come home with us so we know you're safe."

"Are you sure?" Karli asked.

"Yes. And tomorrow, we'll figure out the next step." Jessica tore her gaze away from Braden. She reached her hand out for Karli.

Karli took her hand and squeezed. It was good to not be alone anymore.

KARLI AND JESSICA spent the day catching up as much as they could with Braden around. He gave them time alone, but Karli was aware he was there the whole time and didn't get into too much with Jessica beyond learning Braden had been there for her the entire time she was running from the police.

Braden cooked them dinner, and the three of them tried

to make a plan. Through it all, Karli knew her best and only option was to get in touch with Cade Murray. She didn't know much about him, but she trusted Frannie and Marcus. Marcus was the police captain, and if he said Cade was a real PI, Karli would let him help her, and in turn, she would help him.

Karli settled in Braden's guest room and tried to relax. She'd showered and changed into borrowed clothes from Jessica, but she still felt off. She didn't like being in Braden's house. Not because she didn't trust him, but because she knew being there put Braden and Jessica at risk.

Muffled laughter from Braden's room made her smile. Jessica had been in love with Braden for years, and for them to be together and happy made Karli believe everything would work out in the end. Jessica survived being framed for murder, and she found a way to connect with Braden through it all.

When they got to his house, Braden went to fix up the guest room, which Karli assumed was the first of many ways to give Jessica and Karli a minute alone. Jessica shared that Braden sought her out when she was running. Jessica had to hide her face, so she stayed in parks and on benches until Braden took her to a safe house. Jessica felt guilty that Karli was on her own, too. Karli assured her there was no way she could have known what was really going on. They cried and agreed they would do whatever they needed to do to find out what was really going on, and find Tonya's cousin and save her from Damon. Save everyone from Damon.

Karli couldn't stop thinking about Tonya. She didn't appreciate the woman breaking into her apartment, but that didn't mean she deserved to die. Especially the way she was killed. The brick Karli treasured from her grandfather was a piece she'd never be able to look at again because it was used to take a woman's life. A woman who was just trying to find someone she loved.

Soft moans from the bedroom had Karli stuffing the pillow over her head. She waited, happy for her friend but not really wanting to have inside knowledge of her relationship. When she thought it was safe, Karli removed the pillow and sighed. The house was quiet.

Every little noise stole Karli's attention. She hadn't had a full night of sleep in weeks, and she was not only scared, but she was sure her hell wasn't over. Not by a long shot.

DAMON STREET PACED in front of his desk at the warehouse. He was waiting for a visitor. He needed confirmation the little fucker didn't rat him out. The last thing he could handle was the police having confirmation about who he was.

A firm knock on the door brought his head up. "Yeah?"

The door swung open. Mick met Damon's gaze. It wasn't a look Damon liked seeing on his bodyguard's face. Usually that look said Damon wasn't going to be happy with whatever Mick had to tell him.

"You have a visitor."

"Good. Finally."

Mick gave a slight shake of his head. Enough that Damon saw it but no one else would. Subtle. Mick didn't want whoever was standing next to him to see the silent signal.

Damon straightened and crossed his arms. He leaned back and waited.

Mick stepped back and opened the door all the way. He stared at the visitor until the man stepped into view.

Damon scowled.

"Lovely to see you, too, Damon."

"What the fuck do you want, Trevor?"

"I've been sent by the boss."

Damon did his best not to let his emotions show. It had been a hell of a fucking day, and now the boss was pulling this fucking shit. "Why?"

"It seems you haven't been living up to your responsibilities lately. I've been asked to intervene."

"Fuck you," Damon blurted. He hated Trevor. They'd worked together since they were barely old enough to drive, and Trevor had always been a fuckwad with his nose pressed up someone's ass. Back in the day, Damon worked with Trevor's older brother, Clyde. The three years between them were enough that Damon knew Trevor was a waste of fucking space back then. Trevor tried to hang around with him and Clyde, but all he ever did was fuck things up worse. Why the boss kept him around was something Damon would never understand.

Trevor chuckled at Damon's outburst. The weaselly son-of-a-bitch looked around Damon's office like it was beneath him to even be there. His dark hair was slicked back and his diamond earrings sparkled with the same shine. His nose had a kink in it, one Damon was quite proud of after delivering the blow that broke the little fucker's nose when Trevor was only seventeen.

But now... Now, Trevor was in Damon's office with orders from the boss. Orders that would have been handed directly to Damon just a week or two ago, but were being delivered by Trevor.

"Are you an errand boy?" Damon taunted him.

"I'm whatever I need to be to make sure shit gets done and the boss is happy. Isn't that the job we all have?"

Damon grunted.

"Only problem is it seems you haven't been doing much of that lately. Bringing in outsiders to take care of things that never should have been Company business."

"Fuck you."

Trevor chuckled again. "No, thanks. I hope that piece of ass you're chasing is worth it because she's making you look like the fucking pussy I always knew you were."

Damon lunged at him and swung.

Trevor stepped out of his way, letting Damon nearly fall to the floor when his momentum carried him over.

"I'm going to break your nose again."

"No, you're not, because if I go back to the boss like that, you know you won't survive the night."

Damon growled. He hated it, but it was true. If the boss sent Trevor there, it meant Damon was on the shit list and Trevor was the new favorite.

"Good. Now, you have to clean up the mess you made."

"What mess?"

"Well, aside from the storm you brought and the unnecessary attention the Company has been getting, you need to tie up loose ends."

"What fucking loose ends?"

"The cop."

"What are you talking about?"

"God, you're so fucking stupid. You have someone. The boss knows it. Has known it for years. It has to end."

"Why the fuck would I do that?" Damon swallowed roughly. He didn't think anyone knew he had a cop on his own personal payroll.

"Because you're being ordered to!" Trevor shouted.

Mick burst through the door, eyes blazing as he looked between the two men.

Trevor pulled a gun from behind his back and pointed it at Mick. "You have five seconds to walk back out that fucking door before this carpet will be stained with whatever fucking color makes up the inside of your stupid fucking head."

Mick glared at Trevor but left, closing the door with a solid thud that echoed through the mostly empty warehouse so late at night.

Trevor kept the gun trained on the door a minute longer, then swung his gaze to Damon.

"You fucked up. That's all that matters here. You fucked up, and now you have to fix it. I don't give a fuck about your ex or how stupid she's making you look. I care about what you're doing to the Company and the boss. It stops now."

"Aw, look at you being the protective lap dog you are."

Trevor glared at Damon. Trevor might be able to scare Mick, but nothing scared Damon. Not some stupid fucking prick who wouldn't even be working for the Company if it weren't for his brother. When Clyde died, Trevor took advantage and talked the old boss into giving him a shot at Clyde's old job. Trevor was enough of a kiss-ass that he held onto the job. Years later, he was still a fuck-up, but he was a fuck-up who had the support of the boss, apparently.

"The cop needs to go," Trevor said.

"Fuck you."

"Fine. You don't want to do it, you know someone else will."

"You don't even know who it is."

"You think I won't figure it out?"

Damon snorted. "I know you won't. You're too fucking stupid. No one knows who it is."

Trevor nodded. "You know this is a direct order. The cop dies. Everyone involved in your secret little project to get back your ex needs to go. The cop took care of the guy who killed the friend, and now you need to take care of the cop. No strings."

"There aren't any strings. None of this comes back to the Company."

Trevor descended on Damon so fast he didn't have time to move out of the way. Trevor pinned his arm behind his back and slammed his face onto the desk. Damon heard the door open, and the click of a gun being cocked.

"Five! Four!" Trevor shouted.

The door closed again.

The cold steel pressed against Damon's head. He'd never been afraid of death. He knew it was coming for him. A person didn't choose the life he had without being prepared for death every minute of every day.

But he was not going to die at the little piss-ant's hand. Not now, not fucking ever.

Damon struggled against Trevor, finding the man stronger than Damon expected. Two decades ago, it was easy to toss Trevor around. Now, the man had more strength than Damon gave him credit for.

"Wouldn't want to slip and accidentally shoot you in the fucking head," Trevor taunted, digging the edge of the gun into Damon's temple.

"Fuck you, Trevor. You're not man enough to fucking kill me. You know the boss will be pissed."

"The boss has given me power to do whatever I see fit to clean up the mess you've made. Under your watch, we missed shipments, lost product, and almost lost an asset. You've cost the Company money, and the boss is pissed. If I came back covered in your blood, I might get a promotion."

Damon struggled again, but Trevor didn't budge.

"Take care of the cop. Clean up your fucking act. And

next time you're told to do something, show the fuck up. I won't be back asking nicely."

Trevor shoved at Damon, then released him. Trevor turned and walked toward the door. Damon scrambled around his desk for the gun he kept in his top drawer. He'd just grabbed it when a shot rang out, close enough that Damon felt the air move next to his head.

He looked up and found Trevor pointing his gun at him. The end was smoking.

"Don't you ever try to shoot me when my back is to you."

Damon glared at him.

A minute later, Trevor slid his gun back into the back of his pants and let himself out of the office.

Another minute later, Mick came in. "What the fuck was that all about?"

"Trevor's the new second, apparently."

"What?"

Damon glared at the door. "That was my notice. The boss isn't happy. And neither am I."

5

———

"ARE YOU SURE YOU DON'T WANT US TO COME IN WITH YOU?" Jessica asked. The worry was written all over her face. So was exhaustion. She'd been through her own kind of hell the last few weeks. Karli couldn't ask more of her.

"I'm sure," Karli said. "I will be fine. He wants the same thing I do."

"We think. You said he's convinced Raina knows something."

"Yeah, but he doesn't know what or if she does know anything. He's even more in the dark than I am. He needs my help, and I want to help him," Karli said. She unbuckled her seatbelt and reached for the handle.

"Is he cute?" Jessica asked.

Karli breathed a laugh even as her entire body heated. She didn't want to look at Cade when they met, but she would have to have been dead to not notice how attractive he was. It was good she sort of was dead. Then she could play it off and tell herself there was no chance.

"He's good looking," Karli admitted. "But that doesn't matter."

"It always matters," Jessica said with a smirk.

"Should I be here for this conversation?" Braden asked, winking at Jessica.

Jessica looked over at him with a dopey gaze that promised far more nights like the one they had.

A pang of jealousy landed squarely in Karli's chest. She didn't want to be jealous of them, but she was. Their hell was over. Jessica was cleared. She didn't kill anyone. Karli was the one who was still in hiding. Until she could figure out who Tonya was and where her cousin was.

"I'll let you guys know how everything goes," Karli said, breaking the trance the two lovebirds were in. "Thanks for letting me stay with you last night."

"You can still stay with us," Braden insisted. He tried to convince her earlier that staying with them was a good idea, but Karli turned it around and reminded him that Jessica just got her life back. Karli wasn't going to risk endangering her. Braden got it, but he clearly didn't like it.

"If I have no other option, I'll let you know. I'm hoping Mr. Murray will figure out something for me. It's in his best interest to do so."

Jessica got out of Braden's truck and hugged Karli tight. "Please be careful. We'll wait here for a little while to make sure you're good. If you don't come back in ten minutes, we'll assume he agreed to help you."

"Sounds good. Thank you. Go be happy."

Jessica chuckled. "I'll be happy when all of this is over and you and Raina are safe."

"The only way to make sure that happens is to take down Damon."

"Then that's what we'll do."

Karli nodded at Jessica's confidence. Karli wished she had that same backbone. The one that held her up a little straighter and made her believe it would all be okay. The first sign of danger and Karli snuck out the window. She wasn't strong or badass like her friend. She was scared.

Karli forced herself to walk up to the office building. It was a single story brick building that was probably a home at some point. It appeared as though Murray Investigations was the only place that occupied the space. There was no doorbell, and when she reached for the doorknob, it turned easily.

She took a breath and stepped inside. She forced a smile for Jessica, then closed the door behind herself. She took a few steps forward into the reception area.

"I'll be right there," a man called from somewhere else in the building.

Karli was fairly sure it was Cade's voice, but fear pulsed through her veins and told her to get the hell out of there. Jessica and Braden were still outside. She could just turn around and leave and tell the police she was still alive and it would all be over.

Except it wouldn't be.

Tonya was dead because Damon's hitman thought she was Karli. If Karli made it public that she was alive, Damon might send someone else after her. Or after Jessica. Or Raina. There was very little doubt all of this was about Damon getting Raina back. He was the kind of man who didn't like to be wrong, and didn't like to be outsmarted.

Raina running for her life and getting away from Damon made him look foolish. And if he was the man it seemed he was, the only way for Damon to recover would be to rectify the situation. Which likely meant killing Raina.

"How can I... Karli," Cade said.

He was even more attractive than Karli remembered, and her long neglected body took notice. Dressed in a light gray button-down shirt and black dress pants, he could have been a lawyer or a doctor. His sleeves were rolled up and showed off muscled forearms covered in dark hair. His hair was cut short on the sides and slightly longer up top, like a military haircut but with a little more fashion. His full beard was neatly trimmed and the same dark shade of brown as his eyes.

"Are you here to turn yourself in?" Cade asked, crossing his arms over his thick chest.

Emotion backed up inside her as she imagined him folding her up in those arms. She couldn't remember the last time she'd been held by a man. God, she really needed to start dating again. Once her life wasn't teetering on the edge of a fucking disaster.

Cade raised a brow, and she snapped out of her stupor.

"I'm here because I think we can help each other."

"Really?"

Karli forced a bravado she didn't feel and mimicked his wide stance. "Yes. We both want the same thing. And it makes sense to work together."

"You want to prove your friend killed Tonya?" he asked, his voice incredulous.

"No. I want to take down the person who did. I'm assuming you're interested in the truth, or maybe I'm mistaken about who you are."

He scowled and dropped the smirk. "I've only ever been after the truth."

"Good. Then we're on the same side."

He held her gaze for a long minute, then sucked in a breath. "Fine. I need to know where Raina is."

"She's gone. Left town. Went to stay with family. When she thought I was dead, she figured it was Damon who came after me, after her. She disappeared." The lie came easily enough for Karli. She refused to put Raina in anyone else's crosshairs, good guy or bad.

"Dammit. Do you have a way to get in touch with her?"

Karli held up her hands. "I don't have a phone."

"Why not?"

"It was in my apartment. So unless you want me to walk into the police station and tell everyone I'm alive—"

"Fuck," Cade growled.

"Exactly. But Raina wasn't involved with this. She had nothing to do with Tonya's death."

"How do you know that? Did you speak to her?"

"I did, but I also know her. She's my friend. She lived with me. I trust her, and I know she's not a violent person. She never would have hurt someone unless her life depended on it, and even then, probably not."

"But you aren't sure?"

"When I left my apartment, Tonya was the only one there. I can't say for sure what happened, but the police arrested the guy who killed Tonya. Why do you still think Raina had anything to do with it?"

"It's awfully convenient he's dead now."

"It is. But from what Raina told me about Damon, he's an evil bastard, so I guess it's not a shock. Silver admitted to Jessica that he killed Tonya."

Cade blew out a breath. "But he did it on Damon's orders?"

Karli nodded. "That's what he told Jessica."

Cade ran a hand over his beard and down his neck. He paced away from Karli, deeper into the office building. She stayed rooted to her spot, unsure if she was supposed to follow him or if he was coming back.

"Dammit!" he shouted from down the hall.

Karli jumped and nearly ran out the front door.

Cade turned and came back toward her. His gaze was sharp, but not cruel. He looked defeated. Like he had come so close but lost it all.

"If we know who killed Tonya, and we know Damon put him up to it, and we believe Damon was involved in kidnapping Edie, and the only thing Damon cares about is Raina, we need Raina to help us."

"You're not using my friend as bait."

"I didn't say that. I just said she needs to help us. Unless she's still involved with him and a part of this."

"Not a chance. Raina hates him. She blames herself for all of this. She's terrified and wants Damon to pay for everything he's done."

"Then maybe she can call him. Make him think she's willing to go back to him in exchange for Edie. You said she's not in the area, but he doesn't know that."

"It's too dangerous. I'm not going to risk Raina's safety."

"You said you wanted the same thing I do."

"I do. I want to send Damon Street to jail. He deserves to rot away for the rest of his life."

"He deserves so much worse than that," Cade growled.

"I'm not going to disagree, but I'm also not willing to go to jail for killing him."

Cade snarled. "He doesn't deserve to live when he can discard a life so easily."

"We're not going to get anywhere like this. Do you want my help? Do you want to find Tonya's cousin and prove Damon was the one responsible for Tonya's death?"

"Yes," Cade said.

"Good. Then we can work together. But I have one condition."

"I can't tell the cops you're alive?" Cade asked with a smirk.

"Okay, two conditions. That and I need protection."

"Excuse me?"

"Protection. I need somewhere safe to stay. I can't stay with any of my friends right now because I don't want to risk their safety, and I can't go home. Do you have somewhere I can stay where I'll be safe?"

Cade didn't answer, just stared at her for a long moment.

Karli's confidence slipped. She opened her mouth to tell him to never mind and she'd figure it out when he spoke.

"You can stay with me."

"With you?"

Cade shrugged. "I don't have a safe house I could leave you in, and even if I did, I wouldn't be able to leave you there alone. So, since my safety is clearly not a concern, you can stay with me."

That was not what Karli was expecting, but she had to admit it made sense. Jessica went to a safe house, but she went with Braden. And she was monitored by Taylor's boyfriend and his team. She was never alone.

"Okay," Karli said. She had no other options, so she accepted.

"Now, tell me everything you know about Damon Street and Raina London."

Karli nodded. "Should we go to your office?"

CADE GLANCED BACK at Karli half a dozen times before they made it down the hall to his office. He was sure she was going to turn around and leave like she did the last time he saw her.

Fucking hell, he couldn't believe his luck. He had been looking for her since she disappeared at the high school, and she just walked in like she had an appointment. Jesus, his heart was still pounding.

And it had nothing to do with how sexy she looked in those leggings that hugged her curves.

He was not in a position to get involved with anyone. And definitely not someone like her, who was supposed to be dead and wanted dead by one of the most ruthless men in the city.

Cade waited for her to walk into the office, then closed the door behind them. He walked around his desk and took his seat, cringing when his old chair creaked under his weight. He needed to replace it before the frame gave out on him, but money was tighter than usual lately and it was all he could do to pay his bills.

"Where do you want to start?" Cade asked, pulling out a recording device.

"What's that?" Karli asked, pointing to the recorder that was almost as old as Cade.

"I don't trust recording on my phone because someone could steal it."

"You're going to record this?"

"I'm guessing you'd rather I didn't."

"Um, yeah." She was cute when she was flustered.

No. He was not going to think about her that way. He cleared his throat and stuffed the recording device back into the drawer. He pulled out the legal pad he'd been making notes on since Tonya first walked into his office and a pen and looked up at Karli.

"Where do you want to start?" he repeated.

Karli drew a breath, capturing Cade's gaze with the rise of her breasts as they strained against the tee she wore. He forced himself to look away and focus on the pen in his hand instead of the way his pants tightened.

"Raina and I went to college together. We met in our freshman English class and realized we lived in the same dorm. We got to know each other and ended up rooming together after that."

Cade scribbled as she spoke, not knowing what might matter later.

"When we graduated, we lost touch. I moved to California, and Raina ended up here. I've only been back about eighteen months, but when I moved back, I learned Raina was here. We connected, but she was dating Damon and he was controlling her time. I didn't think much of it at the time since it had been years since we'd seen each other. If I'd known…"

"What happened?" Cade asked. It didn't take a psychologist to figure out something bad happened and Karli blamed herself.

"Damon was abusive. Raina said at first it was little things, but over time it got worse. She finally left when he almost killed her. But that was after he'd broken bones and forced himself on her and threatened to kill her if she didn't behave."

"Fuck," Cade hissed.

"Yeah. Raina went to a shelter for a few months. When she got out, she moved in with me."

"Which is why Damon wanted you dead," Cade finished.

"Exactly. He must have found out Raina was staying with me. She said she never mentioned me to him because he didn't care about her friends or her life, but he obviously found out."

Cade sucked in a breath and leaned back in his chair. It creaked again, prompting him to launch himself forward before it gave out. "But he had a man who lived in your building kill Tonya. Who was he?"

Karli shook her head. "I don't know. I'd seen him a few times, but I didn't know him. Jessica said she spoke to him. His name was Silver Jones, and it sounds like he was a psychopath. He told her he'd killed a lot of people, women it sounded like. He said he would have raped Tonya if he thought he had time. I think that was his usual."

"Jesus," Cade whispered. Bile rose in his throat. He knew Damon was evil, but he had no idea it was that kind of evil. If this guy was a lackey for Damon, Cade didn't want to imagine the kind of things Damon himself did.

Karli sighed heavily. "I know you knew Tonya, and I'll be honest and say I'm struggling a bit. She did break into my apartment. I'm sorry she's dead, and I feel guilty being happy it wasn't me, but she broke in."

"That didn't mean she deserved to die," Cade blurted. Tonya was in pain. She was desperate to find her cousin. She knew something horrible happened to Edie and was only looking for answers. Tonya believed Edie was dead, but she needed to know the truth. She wanted to take down whoever had a hand in her cousin's disappearance, but she wasn't a bad person.

"I never said it did. Like I told you before, if she'd knocked on the door, Raina probably would have helped her. Raina hates Damon for what he did to her."

Cade nodded. His guilt was guiding him now. If he'd never told Tonya where Raina was, she wouldn't have gone there. They were supposed to go together once Cade had proof she was there and that her connection to Damon was no longer active, but Tonya was too impatient. And instead of getting the answers she desperately wanted, she got killed.

And it was Cade's fault.

"If Tonya was killed to try to get to Raina, then Raina is the reason for all of this. I would really like to speak to her."

"That's not an option," Karli said firmly. Again.

Cade knew Raina was the key, and even if she told Karli she didn't know anything about Damon's organization, Cade believed Raina knew something. She had to. She lived with the man. She was his. He had to have said something or done something when she was around. Even if she knew where he worked, it was more than Cade had.

But he had to talk to Raina to get the information.

"Fine, then what can you tell me about Damon?"

"I've never met him, but he's pure evil. From what Raina said, when people he worked with came over, he forced her to stay in the bedroom. If she made any noise, he'd punish her. She tried to listen, but she couldn't ever hear anything, and he locked her inside so she never saw anything."

"Dammit," Cade shouted. "There has to be something. He's been tied to cases for years. There's no way a man like him is innocent, or that he is good enough to have covered his tracks. Someone has to know something."

"I agree. And I think it's up to us to figure out who. But I know it isn't Raina."

Cade studied Karli for a minute. She was determined to keep her friend out of this. He admired her commitment to Raina. Karli was the kind of friend everyone should have. The kind of friend who would let a person know when they were about to step into a pile of shit. The kind of friend Cade could have used before his career and life went belly-up and he almost lost everything.

But this case would change all of that. It would be the thing that proved he was good at what he did. He just had to find all the missing pieces. Starting with Raina London.

6

———————

Karli was exhausted. They'd been going in circles all day. The only thing they'd figured out was that Cade was determined to talk to Raina, and Karli was not telling him a thing about her.

If Raina knew anything, she would have come forward. She would have told Marcus or even Karli, but Raina didn't know anything about Damon or his organization. Karli refused to let Cade, or anyone, threaten Raina or make her feel like she was just as guilty as the monster she once thought she loved.

"We're getting nowhere," Cade said, sounding as exhausted as Karli felt. "I think we need to call it quits for tonight and start fresh tomorrow."

Karli nodded. "Sounds good to me."

"Let me pack up my things and we can go. Any food choices you're opposed to? I usually order something on my way home and pick it up."

"I'm good with anything," Karli said. All Karli cared about at the moment was she would have a safe place to sleep. For the second night in a row. At least, she hoped it was safe. People knew she was with Cade, and if anything happened to her, they would know to come after him.

Cade nodded.

"I'm going to use the restroom before we go."

"Down the hall on the left," Cade said.

Karli left him in his office and went to the bathroom. It was small, but it was clean and uncluttered. When she was done, she heard Cade on the phone and wandered out to the room at the front of the office.

There were a few comfortable chairs and a small desk that Karli assumed was once for an assistant. Karli had been there all day and not only had no one showed up, but Cade hadn't gotten any phone calls. How good of a PI was he if no one needed his services?

She started to wonder if he was who she thought he was. Could he have been someone working for Damon who was pretending to be Cade Murray? Could this have all been a mistake?

Marcus said he knew Cade and said the man on the website was actually him, but what if Damon got to him? What if he was pretending to help but was really helping Damon? What if Tonya was killed because she figured out that Cade wasn't a good guy?

She sat down at the desk and lifted the receiver to check in with Marcus. Maybe he could give her a little more reassurance. The phone on the desk connected to the same line Cade was on. Karli was about to hang up when she stopped.

"Be there in twenty minutes," Cade said.

"And you'll bring her?" the other man asked.

"Yes, but you can't make it too obvious."

"Make sure she comes inside."

Cade sighed. "I will. See you soon."

Did that mean he wasn't sure about turning her over to

whoever he was on the phone with? Or did that mean he wasn't looking forward to running errands for them?

All Karli knew was it meant she had to get the hell away from him. Now.

"Ready to go?" Cade asked, scaring Karli.

She jumped up from the desk and screamed. "Shit!"

"Sorry. I thought you heard me coming. I just ordered food. It's a little Japanese place not far from my apartment. I hope you'll like it."

Karli's head spun. She had to figure out a way to get away from him before he handed her over to Damon and his people. If she'd been paying attention, she could have run out before he got out there, but now she was stuck. If she ran, she had no doubt he'd be able to catch up to her easily.

But she wasn't going to go willingly.

Karli forced a smile for Cade and let him lead her out of the building. He stopped at the front porch, blocking her escape while he locked the front door. She looked up and down the street and found it painfully deserted.

"That's my vehicle," Cade said, pointing to an old blue SUV that looked like it was older than Karli.

"Seriously?"

Cade shrugged. "It works. Most of the time."

Karli studied him while they walked the few steps from the front door to the vehicle on the curb. He didn't look like the kind of man who would turn her over, but Karli didn't have a lot of experience with deceitful criminals. She hated that she chose to trust him and was wrong. She really did want to find out who Tonya was and find her cousin, and take down Damon.

If any of that story was even true.

Cade unlocked the door at Karli's side, opening the door

for her and standing there while she got in. He was smarter than she gave him credit for.

When she sat in the vehicle, he closed the door, then locked the vehicle again. He jogged around the front and unlocked his door, then slid into the vehicle, all before Karli could figure out how to unlock her door and get out.

He pulled away from the curb and a knot twisted in Karli's stomach. No matter what, she was not going into the restaurant with Cade. It didn't matter what he said or did, she was not going inside.

"Are you from the area?" Cade asked as he drove.

"Why?"

"Why?" he echoed.

"Yeah. Why do you care? Why do you want to know?"

He shrugged and let out a frustrated sigh. "I'm just trying to make conversation. Be polite. If we're going to be together twenty-four-seven for a while, I figured I should get to know you."

"Why don't you tell me all about yourself instead?" Karli suggested.

"Okay. I grew up in Texas. I have an older brother who my parents think is God's gift. Jackson, JJ, never did anything wrong when we were kids. He's five years older than me, and I was carted everywhere to follow JJ around. My parents even moved my senior year of high school when my brother decided to leave Texas and move to Colorado. They didn't care that it was my last year of school, they just wanted to be near him."

The tone of his voice said just how much he appreciated that.

"After I graduated, I joined the Army. My grandfather was in the Army, and my grandmother told me stories about him when I was little. My parents didn't care what I did, but they were always proud to tell people my grandfather had been a soldier, so I guess I chose that path hoping they'd give a shit about me. I was wrong."

"That's crappy," Karli said.

"Yep. But I'm too old to give a shit about them now. I'll be forty in six months. I'm living my life for myself now."

"And helping people find lost relatives?" Karli prompted.

Cade gave her a confused look.

"Tonya's cousin? I thought you said she hired you to help find her."

He nodded. "She did, but that's not normally the kind of work I do."

"What kind of work do you do? I thought you were a private investigator." Her throat tightened with fear. Was he really going to admit everything to her? People only did that when they knew the other person wouldn't be around long enough to spill their secrets.

"I usually work with cheating spouses, surveillance, things like that. One on one kind of stuff. To be honest, it's kind of boring work, but it's always paid the bills. Or at least used to."

"It doesn't now?"

"We're here," Cade said, turning off the vehicle before Karli noticed they'd stopped.

He was out of the SUV and opening her door within seconds. She looked up at his offered hand and shook her head. "There's no reason for me to go inside."

"It's not safe for me to leave you out here. If we were followed, it would be easy for someone to yank you out of the vehicle and disappear. I'd never know."

"Were we followed?" Karli asked, her voice pitching high with fear.

"Not that I know of, but it's safer if we stick together. Did you come to me and ask me to keep you safe? I can't do that if I can't keep my eyes on you."

Karli knew he was right, but she hated that she didn't have an argument. Especially one that would get her away from him.

"Why are you doing this?" she asked softly.

"Getting dinner? Because I'm hungry."

She looked up at him with tears in her eyes. "Handing me over to Damon. Why did you lie to me about who you are and tell me you'd protect me if you were just going to let him have me?"

"What are you talking about?"

"I heard you on the phone. He asked if I would be here. Said to make sure I come inside. Is that so I don't scream where someone might overhear and try to stop them from taking me away and killing me?"

Cade's face split into a grin before he threw his head back and laughed. If Karli wasn't so hurt, she might have found the sight of him stunning. He was a beautiful man when he was fierce and determined, but when he laughed, he transformed completely into a man who knew how to enjoy life.

Which apparently meant letting her die and laughing about it.

"Oh, shit, I'm sorry. I shouldn't have laughed, but that was funny." He paused and let out a few more chuckles, still blocking her exit from the vehicle so she couldn't take off down the street and get away from him.

Karli looked past him and found an Asian man and woman standing at the window to the restaurant they were parked in front of. They were both smiling and gesturing to each other, pointing at Cade.

"Who are those people?"

Cade glanced back, and they waved excitedly at him. He groaned and turned to Karli. "That's the Sanos. They own this place. I come here about twice a week on my way home from the office, sometimes again on the weekends. When I called and said I needed to order to-go, Mrs. Sano demanded to know why I wasn't eating inside the restaurant. When I told her I had someone with me and we were going back to my place, she started crying. Mr. Sano was the one you heard on the phone because he insisted I bring you inside so they can meet you."

"Why?"

Cade ran a hand through his short hair. His cheeks darkened ever so slightly with his blush. "They think this is a date. No matter how many times I told them we were working together, they can't be convinced. I told them to not make it obvious they were checking you out because I didn't want to scare you off."

"So, you told them we were on a date and we're having takeout at your place?"

He shrugged and nodded.

"Are you lying to me right now?"

He shook his head. "Karli, you came to me. I was looking for you, but you showed up at my office this morning. You said you looked me up, you did your research. Who else could I possibly be?"

She studied him closely for a minute. After living in LA for years, Karli learned a thing or two about deception. Most importantly was how to read it. It was why she spent the day with him and agreed to go stay with him. At the time, she thought he was an honest person.

"You're sure that's all it is?" she asked.

Cade sighed and nodded. "I promise."

"Okay," Karli said. She drew a breath and took the leap,

choosing, again, to trust the stranger who promised to help her.

CADE WAS EMBARRASSED ENOUGH that the Sanos thought he was on a date, but for Karli to know he had so few that the couple he bought food from every week were excited made him sound like an even bigger loser than he was.

When the truth about Alanna came out, they were the first people to tell him they never liked her. They were polite to her, but in a cold way. Cade got to where he only stopped there for dinner when she was busy and couldn't join him.

He didn't even think about how they would react to him having Karli with him when he went. She was a source, someone helping him on a case. She wasn't a date, even if he did let the Sanos believe it.

Karli got out of the SUV and stood next to him on the sidewalk. He closed her door and locked the vehicle, just in case. They'd only be inside a minute, but if he wasn't watching every second, someone could sneak into the back-seat and put a gun to his head as he drove away. He wasn't taking that chance.

Mr. and Mrs. Sano disappeared from the front window by the time they made it to the door. Karli stepped inside first, waiting for him just inside the door.

They'd barely taken a step forward when Mrs. Sano was on top of them.

"Good evening. How are you tonight?" she asked.

"We're excellent," Karli said. She beamed at Mrs. Sano and stepped closer to Cade. She slid her arm around his waist and her other hand across his chest.

Mrs. Sano's eyes popped wide, and a smile broke out on her face. "Good, good. It's so nice to meet you."

"I'm Karli," she said, resting her head on Cade's shoulder.

"Good to meet you. Cade is a favorite customer of ours. We're happy he's found someone. You're nicer than his last girlfriend."

Karli laughed. "You're not the first person to tell me that. What a piece of work she was. But he finally came to his senses and asked me out."

Cade looked between them and wondered if he was having a stroke.

Mrs. Sano giggled, actually fucking giggled, and reached for Karli's hand. "Oh, I'm so happy. You're such a nice girl. Cade deserved someone nice."

"I'm not always nice," Karli said with a wink that set Mrs. Sano off.

"What's going on over here?" Mr. Sano asked, carrying a bag of food and setting it down on the table behind the host stand.

"Oh, I've just met Karli. She's wonderful. So much better for our Cade than that last girl," Mrs. Sano said.

Mr. Sano grinned. "Is that right?"

"It's so nice to meet you," Karli gushed. "Cade's told me all about the two of you, and I couldn't resist asking him to order from here for our date tonight. I wish we could stay, but I'm having trouble keeping my hands off of him."

She slid her hand up and around his neck and pulled him down. The sneaky look in her eyes said she was enjoying the game she was playing.

She smirked at him just before her hands tugged him to her and their lips collided. She gasped, like she hadn't meant for it to go so far, but Cade's caveman brain kicked in and took over.

He had a beautiful curvy woman in his arms with her lips pressed against his. There was only one answer to that. Only one thing to do. Only one option when a spark lit between them and Cade went hard in an instant.

His arms wrapped her close. His hands splayed wide on her back. He teased the seam of her lips with his tongue and she gasped again, opening for him to take advantage of her surprise.

Then she licked his tongue, and it was game fucking on.

He growled and let her feel how hard he was before a throat was cleared loudly and the two of them separated like teenagers caught beneath the bleachers.

"Well, I can see why you wouldn't want to have dinner here. Maybe you can save some of that dessert for later," Mr. Sano said.

Karli dabbed at her lips and smiled shyly at him. "I apologize. I did not mean for that to happen."

Mr. Sano grunted. "It's not you who should be apologizing. Cade should be respectful of you and treat a woman like a queen. That includes not manhandling her in public."

"You're right," Cade said. "I shouldn't have done that." He looked at Karli, meeting her heated gaze with his own. "I apologize."

Her lips lifted in an unsteady smile. She nodded.

"Leave them be," Mrs. Sano spoke up. "You remember what it was like to be so crazy in lust we could barely keep our hands off of each other. That's what makes a good relationship a great one. You don't want to be wondering what brought you together when you're old. You want to be grabbing each other and losing your mind once in a while. Like we did in the kitchen last week."

It was Mr. Sano's turn to look embarrassed. "We don't need to tell everyone about that."

Mrs. Sano waved her hand. "Oh, psh. I'm not sharing details. Just telling them to enjoy it and never stop enjoying it."

"On that note, I think we should go," Cade said. He handed over a hundred dollar bill and grabbed the food and Karli's hand before Mrs. Sano could make change for him.

Cade ushered Karli into the SUV and set the food at her feet. He locked the doors and hurried around, unlocking them and pulling out onto the road before Mrs. Sano chased him out of the restaurant and tried to give him change.

"They were wonderful," Karli said a minute later.

Cade nodded. "They are. Some of the best people I know."

Karli nodded, then stayed silent for the rest of the drive.

Cade wanted to know what she was thinking, and if it was the same thing he was thinking. That he wanted more of those kisses. As often as possible.

7

———————

Karli kicked herself all through dinner for kissing him. She was trying to play a role and pretend they were on an actual date. She thought it would be a quick peck on the lips and nothing more. But the second their lips brushed, she knew she was in trouble. The kind of trouble that had her silently wishing for more than either of them had to offer.

Okay, so he was seriously attractive, and his focus and determination were two qualities she admired in him, but her life was in shambles. She was hiding out at his apartment because she couldn't go back to her own. She was possibly being hunted by a crazy man who would kill without a thought. Starting anything was the worst of the worst ideas.

But as she ate her dinner and her thigh brushed against Cade's where they sat on his well-worn soft leather couch, she struggled to remember all of that.

"How's your food?" he asked.

"Great. Good. You're perfect. I mean, the food is perfect. It was a really good choice."

Cade nodded and held her gaze for a long moment.

Karli couldn't seem to figure out how to look away from him. It was like being stuck in a trance, staring at his eyes and wondering what he was thinking.

"Should we talk about what happened?" he asked. He grimaced with the words, like it was the last thing he wanted to do.

"You mean when I kissed you?"

He rubbed the back of his neck and nodded. "Yeah. I mean, it was..."

"Part of the story," she blurted, doing her best to save face before he told her it was a mistake and wouldn't happen again. Her cheeks burned with shame at being so quickly dismissed. He was gorgeous, and she was just a curvy art therapist who did not match with him at all. He was muscles and badass, and she was curves and scaredy cat. Nothing about them said they'd be a good pair.

Except the heat Karli felt when they kissed. But that was obviously one-sided.

"Part of the story?" Cade asked slowly, like he didn't believe the lie.

"Yeah. You said they thought we were on a date. I figured it would be more convincing if I was acting like that. If I kissed you. It didn't mean anything." Karli shrugged, doing everything to play the whole thing off as no big deal while her insides shook and demanded a repeat, just to see if that fire between them could be stoked again.

"Didn't mean anything?"

Was he going to repeat everything she said as though it was a question?

"I wanted it to be convincing."

"It sure was that," Cade snarled.

"I guess I should have said something to you before

kissing you like that. I didn't think it would be a big deal. I apologize. It won't happen again."

"It won't?"

Karli shook her head and stood. "No. I promise you. I will not kiss you again." Karli shoved her to-go container into the trash with a little more force than necessary and tried to stop the feeling inside her that said she was dumb to think what she assumed was an erection actually meant Cade was turned on by kissing her. He was just playing along, even if he wasn't in on the game to start with. He picked it up and ran with it, convincing everyone, including her, that it was real.

"Okay, I guess," Cade said.

He remained on the couch, not far from the kitchen in his apartment. It was smaller than hers, but not messy. He kept it clean and organized. As far as she could tell, there was only one bedroom and one bathroom, which meant close quarters. Even closer after Karli kissed him and twisted everything up.

"Is it okay if I take a shower?" Karli asked.

"Um, yeah. Of course. Let me show you where everything is. Do you have... I mean, do you need to borrow something to wear?" His question came out like he choked on the words.

"I have a few things in the bag I brought. Jessica loaned me some stuff, too. I washed it all yesterday, so I'm good. But thanks."

Cade cleared his throat and nodded. He led the way to the bathroom and showed her how to use the shower and pointed out where extra bath products were if she wanted to use anything different from what he had in the shower.

"I'll grab stuff from my room so you can sleep in there.

I'll take the couch," Cade said before he turned to leave the bathroom that was barely big enough for both of them.

"You don't have to do that. I didn't intend to kick you out of your room."

He shook his head. "I would never make you sleep on the couch. Besides, I sleep there half the time, anyway. It's not a big deal."

"Okay," Karli said. "Thanks."

Cade nodded. His gaze slid down her body before snapping to her face. He looked pained again, like he was regretting having her there. "I'll be out here if you need anything. I mean, if... I'm going to go."

Karli watched him close the door and wondered what in the hell that was all about.

CADE RESTED his hands on either side of the doorframe and listened as Karli turned on the water. His fingers turned white as he resisted the urge to open the door and walk right back into the bathroom, but he wasn't that big of an asshole. Especially after she made it clear what he felt during that kiss was not returned.

He felt like an idiot, but he wasn't going to let it get to him. He had a job to do, one he hadn't done in years. He had someone to protect, to keep safe so he could find out what was going on with Damon Street and the rest of the organization he ran.

Cade pushed away from the bathroom door and stalked to his bedroom. He yanked open the first drawer he came to and slammed it shut again. "Fuck," he growled into the empty space.

He drew a deep breath and let it out slowly. He could not

let his desire mess with his head. Getting involved with Karli was a bad idea, for so many reasons, and she wasn't interested. That was the big one.

He closed his eyes and pushed thoughts of her standing naked in his shower out of his mind. He'd been on the wrong side of a one-sided attraction before, and he got over it. He'd do it again.

Cade listened for the shower and heard it still on so he removed his clothes from the day and tossed them into the hamper in his closet. He pulled on sweatpants and a tee, then grabbed clothes for work the next day. He didn't know what Karli would want to do, but just in case, he needed clothes to go into the office.

He folded everything carefully and set the clean clothes on the end table in the living room. He settled onto the couch and found something to watch while he waited for Karli to emerge from the bathroom.

The door opened a few minutes later and Cade nearly lost it. Steam billowed out of the bathroom ahead of her, the scent of his body wash heavy in the air. She left her small backpack by the bathroom door and walked over to him, her body smelling like him.

He was hard in an instant, his mind conjuring images of her soaping up her soft skin and sliding bubbly hands all over her naked body.

He groaned and coughed to cover up the strangled sound, but not before he drew her attention.

"Are you okay?"

He coughed again and nodded. "Good. Sorry. I was going to watch the news. If that's okay."

She nodded. "I should probably keep up with what's going on."

He changed the channel and settled against the arm of

the couch, as far from her as possible. Every time she shifted, her scent mixed with his body wash met his nose and he ached. Jesus, he ached.

"How did you become a private investigator?" Karli asked during a commercial break.

Cade cleared this throat and shifted toward her, immediately realizing it showed off the tent in his sweats. He shifted away again and shrugged. "After the Army, I wanted to help people. I got a degree in criminal justice, but I didn't love the idea of working for a police department. It didn't suit me. One of my classes brought in people who had criminal justice degrees but were working in different sectors. One of them was a PI. It sounded like a good job."

"What do you like about it?"

"I get to help people."

"Like Tonya?"

He nodded. A pang hit him in the chest. Tonya should still be alive. "Like Tonya. And hopefully her cousin."

"What's the most interesting case you've ever had?"

"This one is high up there," he admitted.

"You mean most of your clients don't end up killed in a case of mistaken identity when you're investigating their missing cousin and a criminal organization that no one seems to know anything about?"

Cade chuckled. "Yeah. Definitely not the usual."

"I'm sorry," Karli said a second later. "I shouldn't be so flippant about a woman being dead. I apologize."

"It's okay. I mean, not that she's dead, but I understand. Tonya was a good person, but she was at the edge of her rope with all of this. She was desperate for answers. She and Edie were close. Best friends growing up. They lost touch a little as adults, but Tonya said she knew something was wrong. That Edie never would have disappeared."

"I can't imagine what it must have been like for her. If something ever happened to my cousin, I'd probably go crazy looking for her."

Cade nodded. "She was so frustrated. No one was willing to help her."

"Except you."

Shame licked at him. Karli thought he was the good guy. That he took the case because he was honorable and kind. That he was in it for all the right reasons.

She didn't know what he'd been through. How his career was teetering on the edge. How he was barely hanging on after he became a joke in the industry.

"I hope we can find Edie. I would really like to help you. If that's okay."

Cade nodded, guilt churning inside him.

"Who was the woman the Sanos were talking about?" Karli asked, yanking him out of his stupor.

"What?"

"They mentioned someone you dated before. They didn't sound like they were fond of her."

"Why do you want to know about her?" Cade jumped up from the couch and stomped his way into the kitchen. He poured himself a glass of water and drank it down while waiting for Karli to explain where her questioning was coming from.

"I was just curious," Karli said after a minute.

"Well, there's nothing to tell. It's over. She's not in my life anymore."

"Did she used to live here? Is that why you have all that extra bathroom stuff?"

Cade swallowed roughly. Alanna barely came over to his apartment when they were together. She always said he needed a nicer place. She was embarrassed by where he lived. Cade didn't care. It was nicer than some of the places he'd stayed in overseas, and it was all he really needed. He tried to make it comfortable for her, but she still refused to spend the night with him. It didn't matter how many fruity, flowery, sickly sweet scents he bought or how many throw pillows he added to the couch. She hated his apartment.

It was the only reason he still lived there. When things ended, he tossed all the things he bought to try to make her stay, but the bathroom stuff he overlooked. By the time he remembered it was underneath the sink and shoved to the back, he no longer cared and ignored it all.

Until Karli shoved it in his face.

"No. She never lived here." He walked back to the couch. He pointed the remote at the TV and turned it off. "I'm pretty tired. I need to get some sleep."

He couldn't look at her. He just stared straight ahead, knowing he was being an ass but unable to change his mood.

After a few seconds, she stood. He allowed himself one glance in her direction. Her hands were linked in front of her. Her face pinched into an uncomfortable attempt at a smile. "Okay, well, good night."

"Night," he grunted.

She turned and walked to his bedroom, closing the door softly.

Cade closed his eyes and counted to twenty. Alanna couldn't do anymore damage to him or his reputation. He wouldn't let her. And that included Karli never knowing he only discovered his girlfriend was screwing someone else because the guy's wife hired him. She'd been cheating right under his nose, and Cade had no clue.

KARLI TOSSED and turned for half the night. When she did fall asleep, she either had disturbing dreams about Tonya's death or disturbing dreams about sex with Cade.

Those were disturbing for a very different reason, though.

Karli woke up grumpy, turned on, and feeling very guilty. The only reason she met Cade was because Tonya was dead. If the other woman hadn't been killed, Karli would never have known Cade existed. It wasn't right that someone had to die in order for them to meet.

Not that anything was going to happen. Karli would take her memories of Cade and disappear one day. But until then, she had to keep her attraction to herself before Cade kicked her out for sexual harassment or something. After she kissed him the day before, then pushed for information about his ex, Karli had a feeling it was going to be a very difficult day.

She heard Cade moving around in the rest of the apartment. She thought about getting up, but speaking to him when she was so tense was not going to be a good idea. When the shower turned on, Karli took advantage of Cade being occupied and slid her hand into her panties, finding her body wet and ready. It only took her about five minutes to orgasm. Plenty when he took a ten minute shower.

Karli laid there until she smelled coffee in the air. She rolled out of bed and put her bra back on under the clothes she slept in, then opened the bedroom door.

Cade was in the kitchen, dressed in a suit and his dress shoes already. He stared at his phone and sipped a cup of coffee.

She padded out to the kitchen and said, "Good morning."

"Morning," he grunted. "There's coffee. I'm leaving for the office in twenty minutes."

"I'll be ready," Karli said.

She drank her coffee quickly and changed into something more appropriate for being out in public. Karli debated leaving her things at his apartment, but after the way their night ended and the morning started, she wasn't sure she'd be returning with Cade at the end of the day.

"What's that?" he barked when she moved toward the door with her backpack.

"It's my stuff."

"Why are you taking it with you?"

She shrugged, feeling less confident in her choice. "I didn't get the feeling you wanted me here."

He sighed heavily and closed his eyes. When he opened them again, his dark gaze held the weight of the world.

"You're staying here until we find Damon Street and whoever else is a part of his organization."

"I'll be fine on my own."

"Karli," he said softly. "Please stay. I apologize for being less than friendly. I don't like to talk about my ex. It's a chapter of my life I'd rather forget even existed."

Karli nodded. "Okay."

Cade held her gaze. "So, you'll stay?"

She nodded again. "I'll stay. For now."

"You'll stay until I know you're safe. I'm not risking losing you, too. Not when I've only just found you."

Karli's chest swelled with his words. A smile curled her lips up.

"I mean, I know you can help me find Edie and take down Damon, so I have to keep you safe. Speaking of which, I think you should use Tonya's phone. Since yours is in police custody."

And there went the good feeling. She was nothing more than necessary. And not only that, but she was just a replacement for Tonya, right down to using the dead woman's phone.

Why did she even think that maybe, just maybe, Cade was actually happy she was in his life? She was a fool.

8

———

Day two at Cade's office was a repeat of day one. Karli and Cade argued about Raina and Damon and talked in circles. Nothing had changed, except on day two, all Karli could think about was how little she knew about what was going on.

"What exactly did Damon Street do?" Karli asked once they ordered lunch.

Cade froze for a second. When he looked up at her from across his cheap wooden desk, all the hairs on the back of her neck stood up.

"He's the worst kind of human. He's evil. He doesn't care who gets hurt or who gets killed. He's willing to do anything to get what he wants."

Karli shivered at the thought of Raina being with him. "Why do you think Raina would protect him?"

Cade shrugged. "Because he's not operating alone. If he was, he would have been caught by now. There are rumors about him that go back years. He's created a criminal underground that's rumored to bring drugs and guns into the area and women and children out of the area."

"Children?" Karli choked.

Cade nodded and wiped a hand down his face. "There's never been any proof of anything, and whenever the police think they have a lead, it disappears. Like the guy who killed Tonya. He would have been able to tell the police where Damon is, where he operates from, what he actually does. But instead, he's dead."

"He died in police custody. Doesn't that make it seem like they're involved."

"That's why this is so fucked up. But if Raina really isn't helping him, why wouldn't she help us?"

"Because she doesn't know anything!" Karli shouted for what felt like the hundredth time.

A knock on the front door had Cade getting up with a frustrated groan. Karli felt the same. If he wasn't willing to believe that Raina didn't know anything, they were never going to make any progress.

Cade came back a minute later with a bag of tacos and burritos they ordered from another restaurant Karli had never heard of. He set the food down on his desk and returned to his seat across from her. He stared at his hands for a long moment before looking up at Karli.

"Raina is the only person I've ever heard of who met Damon Street and lived. I'm sure there are others, but they're all a part of his organization. They won't talk. That means Raina is the key."

"Which is probably why he's so desperate to get her back," Karli whispered.

Cade shook his head. "I'm not entirely sure that's the case. If Raina left him like you said, and she's evaded him for months, he's likely angry, but I'm guessing his people are losing confidence in him. If she knows anything—"

"She doesn't," Karli growled.

"Okay, but if she does, his entire operation is at risk. And if she has any names or knows faces, she can help take down everyone involved with him."

"But she doesn't know anything. She said he wouldn't let her out, and she never saw or heard a thing."

"If that's true, I don't know how we're going to find Edie or Damon Street and prove what he's done."

"How do you usually find people in your cases?"

"The one who hired me knows where to look."

Karli sighed. That was obviously not going to work this time. Tonya was dead, and if she knew where to find her cousin, she never would have hired Cade in the first place.

"How did you find Raina?"

Cade looked up at her, and his eyes brightened. "Police reports. That's where we can find Damon."

"How are we going to do that?"

"Some police reports are public record. Others we would have to request. But if we know what we're looking for, we can find information."

"And do we know what we're looking for?" Karli asked.

Cade nodded. "We do. Let's eat. After lunch, we'll get started."

KARLI WAS BEGINNING to regret her decision to help Cade find Damon. Not because Damon didn't deserve to be caught, or because spending time with Cade was a hardship. Nope, she was regretting it because the more police reports she read, the worse of a human she knew Damon Street truly was.

"How do you know all of these are him?"

Cade shook his head as he stared at the screen. "I don't,

but there's a pattern. If we follow the patterns, we can find him. You said he killed the husband of that other woman, and those records led us to the company Oscar worked for. From there, we were also able to see what other things he was tied to. If I'm right and Oscar was working for Damon, everything he did was likely under orders. Except killing his ex-wife."

"But Damon killed him."

Cade nodded absently.

"This is twisted."

"Yeah," Cade said with a grin.

"Why are you so happy about this?" Karli asked.

Cade finally looked up at her. His smile faded as he took in her expression.

Karli could only imagine what he saw. She felt like she was going to be sick. The reports they were reading showcased the worst in humanity. People who were assaulted and tortured. People who were raped before and after they were killed. People who were left to die a slow death after they were beaten beyond recognition and never identified.

If all of the reports were tied to Damon, Karli was even more surprised that Raina got away from him. And more determined to keep her location private. If anyone had any hint of Raina's whereabouts, she's be dead.

"I'm not happy about what happened to all these people," Cade said softly. "It's disgusting and horrible to even think about. It almost makes me relieved that Tonya died quickly like she did because what could have happened to her is unimaginable. But this information will help us. It means we can find Edie, we can take down Damon. We can stop this kind of thing from happening to other people."

Karli drew a breath and nodded slowly. He was right.

Even if he didn't know Silver's plans for Tonya. "The man who killed Tonya was a serial killer. He told Jessica all about another woman he killed. He said his father went to jail for killing and raping her. She said it was like his calling card. He would have done the same to Tonya, but he knew Jessica was on the way."

Cade groaned and shook his head. "I'll never complain about a boring case with a cheating spouse again. That's shitty behavior, but these kind of people... They don't deserve to live."

"As long as the cheating spouse isn't yours," Karli teased.

Cade's lips tightened into a thin line. His eyes blazed with anger. Before Karli could ask what was wrong, he pushed out of his chair and stalked out of his office without a word.

Karli watched him go and wondered what the hell just happened.

Cade stomped back into his office a minute later. He avoided her gaze and snapped his laptop closed. "We should go. It's getting late."

Karli checked the time on the laptop he'd loaned her for the day. It was an hour earlier than they left the day before. She thought about arguing with him and suggesting they stay a little later, but he was already packing his stuff and shutting down his computer.

She turned off the laptop and handed it to him to store in his desk again. He locked the drawer and ushered her out of the office.

Karli regretted not having brought her things like she planned. If she had, she could have walked away from him in that moment. Something set him off, but she wasn't interested in him treating her like she was an inconvenience or a frustration.

The drive to his apartment was tense and silent. He didn't ask if she wanted to order dinner and didn't stop anywhere to pick something up. He just drove and ignored her like she wasn't even there.

At his apartment, Cade went straight to his room. He closed the door less than gently, sending her a not so subtle message that he didn't want to talk to her.

Karli flopped down on the couch and stewed. The longer he took, the more angry she became. And the angrier she became, the less she was willing to sit there and wait for him to get over himself and treat her like a human again.

"I'm going for a run. Don't open the door for anyone," he barked as he hurried to the front door.

Karli didn't have time to say anything before he was gone, locking the door behind her. She was tempted to open it and yell at him, but she didn't. She couldn't. Someone could be watching. Waiting.

She looked through the peephole and found the hallway outside empty. Cade was already gone, and no one was approaching. But she still didn't feel safe.

Karli turned on the TV so she didn't feel so alone. She found a funny movie and stomped her way into the kitchen. If he wasn't going to feed her, she'd find something to eat.

The petty side of her wanted to cook something for herself only, but she couldn't bring herself to do it. Something upset him, and even though it wasn't fair for him to take it out on her, she wasn't willing to be nasty to him in return.

She baked chicken she found in his freezer and made rice and mixed vegetables to go with it. She was just sitting down on the couch to eat when he walked in the door.

"You cooked?" he asked.

"I was hungry."

"I would have ordered something when I got back."

She glanced at him over her shoulder and nearly swallowed her tongue. His gray tee clung to his muscles like a second skin. His shorts were tight to his legs. His hair was wet and shiny with indents running through it where he'd obviously been running his hands. He was almost impossible to resist. "Now you don't have to."

He nodded. "Thank you." He pointed toward the bathroom. "I'm going to take a shower."

She nodded and turned back to the show she was watching to keep from staring at him. He didn't leave right away, but she refused to look at him again.

The bathroom door finally closed a few minutes later. The water came on seconds after that. Karli finally let out the breath she was holding and put her plate down before her shaky hands dropped it.

A man should not be that stunning. He clearly never stopped the workouts he did in the Army. His body was a work of art. A frustrating, irritating, pain in the ass, but still a work of art.

Karli blew out a breath and closed her eyes. She needed to calm her body down and stop the reaction she had to him. Nothing would ever come of it, and letting it get worse was not going to help.

She picked up her plate again and finished eating. The water still ran in the bathroom, so she fixed him a plate of food and cleaned up the mess she made cooking dinner. She left his plate on the counter and had just returned to the couch when the water turned off.

Not wanting to seem like she was waiting for him, Karli jumped up and grabbed her backpack. She rifled through her stolen items and the things Jessica loaned her and found clothes she could sleep in.

The bathroom door opened while she was stuffing the rest of her things into the bag. She grabbed the whole thing and went toward the bathroom to take her shower, only saying *excuse me* when she stepped around him.

Karli closed the door and made the mistake of looking up as the gap narrowed. Cade was watching her, his gaze unreadable as the door broke their connection and separated them.

She flicked the lock on the door and leaned against it, trying to stop her heart from hammering inside her chest.

Karli took her time in the shower. She didn't really want to spend time with Cade with the way he was acting, and a long, hot, solo shower was a good alternative.

When her skin started to prune, she finally turned off the water and stepped out. She wrapped her body in a towel and dug through the products under Cade's sink. She was afraid to use anything the day before, but after his attitude, she didn't care.

Most of the scents were fruity and flowery, which was not Karli's thing, but there was something that was a little less nauseating. Sandalwood and vanilla. She sniffed it and decided to rub the lotion on her legs and arms. She sat on the toilet while she applied it to her damp skin, then finished getting dressed, tucking the lotion back under the sink so she could find it again.

If she stayed there.

Karli opened the bathroom door and decided to say something to Cade. He owed her an apology. It didn't matter what was going on with him, she deserved one. She wasn't willing to beg, and it didn't count if his apology was forced, but Karli couldn't stay silent any longer.

She set her bag down in his bedroom and went back to

the living room. He was stretched out on the couch, giving her the message he didn't want her there.

Fuck that. She wasn't taking it.

She rounded the couch and positioned herself in front of the TV. If she blocked what he was watching, he'd have no choice but to pay attention to her. She glared at him, and...

He was sound asleep.

One hand rested on his thigh, the other was curled up near his collarbone. His eyes were closed, his long, dark lashes casting shadows on his cheeks. One leg was stretched out, and the other was curled under, like he was trying to make room for her but crashed.

His empty plate was on the coffee table. An empty glass sat next to it. He looked so peaceful.

Karli couldn't bear to wake him up and yell at him. In the days she'd known him, he'd never looked so calm. She wanted to clear the air, but she also wanted him to rest.

She picked up his plate and glass and carried both to the kitchen. She started the dishwasher since it was almost full. She checked that the door was locked and turned off most of the lights in the apartment. Then she went over to Cade.

She turned off the TV and set the remote on the coffee table in front of him. With a light on in the kitchen, he would be able to see it when he woke up. She grabbed the blanket on the back of the couch and unfolded it carefully, draping the fabric over his body so he didn't get cold.

Cade was even more beautiful when he was sleeping. His strong cheekbones and short beard gave him a take-no-shit air. But in sleep, all of it was softened.

Karli looked at his face closely and tried to memorize it. She'd never been so close to him and wasn't sure when she would be again, but she knew she'd never forget him.

Maybe it was wrong, but she wanted the image of him in her memory bank. Something to hold on to when he was no longer a part of her life.

She drew a soft breath and held still, letting the back of her hand brush over his beard. She wondered if it was as soft as it looked and closed her eyes when she found it was.

They snapped back open when his hand closed around her wrist.

"Karli," he groaned, his gaze soft and questioning.

"I'm... I'm sorry," she stammered, trying to pull her arm away.

"I'm sorry. I shouldn't have gotten upset earlier."

She nodded, still trying to escape. She was too close, and he smelled too good, and there was no way he didn't notice she was touching him.

"What are you doing?"

"You fell asleep. I was just covering you with a blanket."

The edge of his lips quirked up. "Is that why you were touching my beard?"

"I shouldn't have done that. I'm sorry."

"I liked it." His voice dipped low, resonating between her thighs and tightening her belly.

"What?"

"Karli," he whispered, tugging her wrist.

She lost her balance and fell onto the couch next to him. His other hand speared into her hair and dragged her body down to his. He rose up to meet her, their lips colliding in the middle.

Cade groaned when they kissed, parting her lips with his tongue without resistance from her. He held her wrist and her head and plundered her mouth with kisses that left her drunk with lust and ready for more.

Karli's brain finally caught up to what was happening,

and she kissed him back. She used her free hand to stroke his beard and pushed her fingers into his short hair. She wanted to explore him, but he gentled their kiss and ended with soft pecks against her lips.

"We should get some sleep," he said, laying back on the couch and releasing the hold he had on her. "Thank you for the blanket."

Karli stood up and stumbled to the bedroom, unable to keep the smile from her lips.

9

CADE'S STOMACH ROLLED AT THE DESCRIPTION HE READ. HE knew Damon Street was bad news, but reading report after report that Cade was sure were tied to Damon drove home just how psychotic the man truly was.

Twelve years in the Army forced Cade into situations beyond normal comprehension. He saw people sacrifice their own children and families in order to protect their country. He saw kids barely bigger than the gun they held shooting as tears streamed down their faces. He saw evil and horror and pain that would never leave his memory. But as horrible as it was, all of it was in the name of freedom. All of the fighting was to try to save or defend something, on both sides. They didn't agree with each other, but both sides thought they were doing the right thing.

With Damon and his organization, there was no rationale. No justification. They were killing people to keep them silent. They were doing things without any reason beyond *because they could.*

Cade had gone back years into the police files, trying to build a picture of Damon Street. The profile he was putting together was someone who was untouchable. There weren't any documented pictures of the man. No one could give a clear description of him. It was obvious he had a network of not just employees but officials in his pocket. From dirty politicians who helped with cover-ups to cops who never investigated crimes. Damon Street was likely behind more unsolved cases than Cade ever imagined.

But the one he was most concerned about was Edie. Tonya trusted him. She wasn't sure about working with him, but he convinced her he would do everything to find her cousin. He told her he'd work around the clock and stop at nothing to find her. And instead of doing that, he got Tonya killed and was shacking up with the woman she was mistaken for.

Cade looked over at Karli, her head bent over the computer she was studying. They'd been working for hours, but Karli hadn't said a word. She hadn't spoken much at all that day.

Cade was still thinking about their kiss the night before. He wondered if she was mad at him for kissing her. She glanced at him, as though she could feel his stare, and her lips curled into a smile. She looked away again, leaving a smile on Cade's face.

She wasn't supposed to be in his life. She wasn't even supposed to be alive. But she was there helping him and being kind to him.

He wasn't sure he'd ever get over the guilt he felt every time he looked at her. When he first saw her, he was almost angry she was alive and Tonya wasn't. Karli was the real target, but Tonya died. She died because Cade made an error and shared information with her. He knew she was going to go there, even though he warned her not to go without him. He should have done more to stop her. Or never told her he found Raina.

But if he had, Karli would be dead.

And that admission started the guilt cycle all over again.

"I need a break," Cade admitted. He stood and stretched, noticing Karli's gaze slid over his body and stalled on his crotch. His cock twitched. The fucker had been demanding since their first kiss in the restaurant and hadn't let up. After their kiss on the couch, his cock was hard more often than not and making him second guess pulling back and telling Karli to go to bed.

It wasn't an easy decision, but when he opened his eyes, he swore she was Tonya, and it made him retreat.

"I think my eyes are permanently crossed from staring at the screen for so long," Karli said. She closed the laptop and pushed it away, stretching her back over the chair. The move popped her breasts up, like she was offering them to him.

His cock liked that a lot.

Cade cleared his throat and shifted his erection. He hurried past her, mumbling something about the bathroom, before slamming himself behind the locked door.

He gripped the sides of the sink and drew in deep breath after deep breath. He needed to get a hold of himself. Fucking hell, he couldn't fuck her over his desk or on the table or anywhere in his office. Not only was it so very wrong, but she deserved better than something like that. Karli was going through hell, and he was an even bigger ass than he already accepted he was if he fucked her in the middle of the mess she was in.

After a few more minutes, Cade finally calmed down enough to leave the bathroom. Karli was in his office, focused on the computer again. Her shoulders were pulled up tight to her ears, tension clear in her entire body.

"Should we get some lunch?" Cade asked.

"Sure. Whatever you want." She didn't look up at him.

"What sounds good today?"

"I'm easy. I'll eat whatever."

He didn't want to groan, but he was frustrated. He put her on edge again. She'd been that way off and on since he shut down on her the night before. When she made a joke about finding his spouse cheating, it hit far too close to home. Not that she knew what she was saying, but it dug under Cade's skin and made him feel like shit.

"Listen, about yesterday," Cade began.

"We don't need to talk about yesterday. We're good." Karli slapped the laptop closed and pressed her lips up into a smile that looked painted on, then walked straight out of his office. Five seconds later, the bathroom door closed and the water turned on.

"Fuck," Cade hissed. He ran a hand through his hair and resisted the urge to punch himself in the throat.

He needed to clear the air with her. Be honest. But first, he needed to order lunch.

KARLI STAYED focused on the computer in front of her during lunch, not looking up at Cade once. He was starting to get annoyed. She could at least speak to him, but every time he asked her something, she returned a one-word answer, if anything.

He finished his food and was ready to confront her when someone walked into the office. He didn't have any other clients and wasn't expecting anyone. His entire body went on alert, tension rolling through his as he prepared for battle and to protect Karli at all costs.

"That's Marcus," Karli said, closing the laptop and standing up.

She moved toward the door, but Cade jumped in front of her. "What if it's not?"

"Who else would it be?"

Cade raised a brow, and Karli reared back like she never considered anyone else would know she was there. She sucked in a breath and nodded for Cade to go out ahead of her.

"Can I help you?" Cade asked Captain Marcus Patrick. He knew who he was, but Cade didn't know if the Captain was one of the cops working for Damon Street.

"Karli said she was staying with you and working here. She asked me to come for a meeting with the two of you at two o'clock."

"Did you come alone?" Cade asked, crossing his arms over his chest and rocking back on his heels. He eyed the other man closely, not caring that he was the police captain and could get him run out of town if he chose. Cade had a job to do, and he wasn't going to let another woman die because of him.

"I did. No one knows where I am. Not even my assistant knows." Captain Patrick met Cade's gaze with a level one of his own. He didn't look bothered by Cade's questions or reluctant to answer.

Cade finally nodded, hoping he was doing the right thing. He jerked his head toward the back, indicating Captain Patrick could follow him.

Cade stepped back from the door and let Karli greet Captain Patrick.

"Thanks for coming, Marcus. I really appreciate your help."

The Captain smiled and pulled Karli into a warm hug.

"Of course. It sounds like you've uncovered a lot more than we have."

"We have the luxury of time. Being dead means I don't have any obligations."

Marcus scowled at her words. "We're going to fix that."

Karli nodded. "Once we get Damon. I don't want to risk him finding out where Raina went. Her family could be in danger, too."

Marcus's brows tugged together for a brief second, then he smoothed his features and smiled. "We'll get him."

"Have you figured out what police officer killed the last witness?"

"Silver James wasn't exactly a witness. He was a suspect." Marcus growled.

"Does that mean you figured out how he was killed?"

Marcus scowled again. He shook his head. "We know someone laced the water bottle he was given, but we haven't figured out who or how. The officer who gave it to him was cleared of all wrongdoing. He's back on duty."

"Seriously?" Cade spat.

"Did I come here for you to tell me I'm not doing my job? Because as far as I've heard, you're having some issues lately," Marcus snapped.

The two men squared off. Cade sneered at the police captain, and Marcus smirked right back at him. In the years he'd been a private investigator, Cade had worked with law enforcement plenty. Usually his cases weren't criminal, but he was happy to share information when he came across anything that could help out. He'd never worked directly with Captain Patrick, but he believed him to be an honest and dedicated man.

But he was clearly willing to play dirty.

"Can we stop measuring dicks over here and talk? We're

on the same side, for crying out loud," Karli barked, stepping between the men. She pushed back on Cade's chest, then immediately dropped her hand like he'd burned her.

Marcus's brow jumped up, but he did as Karli asked and dropped the macho attitude. "She's right. I came here because Karli said you two had some information that might help. She said you've been looking into old cases. Which ones?"

Karli sat at the table she'd been using as a desk for two days and flipped the pages of her legal pad to the front. She spun her computer around to face the other chairs at the table and nodded for the men to sit with her.

Cade shared a look with Marcus. Marcus moved first, taking the seat with the better view of Karli's screen. Cade sulked as he sat in the other chair and tried to see what Karli was presenting.

"We started with what we knew. Silver and Jessica. We looked into that case as much as possible. Then we moved to Oscar and Holly. I looked into Oscar's past and everything else he's been tied to. Then we kept going, looking at any other unsolved cases, or cases that you know what happened but don't have the suspect. Cade gave me some ideas about trends and methods, whether it was the weapon used or the location. Obviously, there's no way for me to know if all of these are Damon or someone who works for him, but these are the cases I think could be tied to him."

Cade peered around the edge of the screen and saw a list of almost thirty cases. His own list was much smaller, but he recognized a few they had in common.

"Not all of these are unsolved," Marcus said, studying the list. "There are some where we have a suspect, just not in custody. Or we know who did it, but we haven't been able to find them."

"What happened to innocent until proven guilty?" Cade asked.

"Innocent people don't disappear for years," Marcus growled. "They don't have the network or the desire to walk away from their lives for something they didn't do. The worst part of my job is knowing I've sent innocent people to jail. I know I have. That's almost worse than knowing we've let criminals walk because we didn't have everything in order. I want to put away anyone who commits a crime."

"What cases do I need to cross off the list?" Karli asked.

Marcus showed her some of them. She argued one or two, but most of them she let go. Until the last one.

"That can't possibly be tied to Damon," Marcus said. His face went white, and his eyes blazed with ghosts from long ago.

"It might not be, but it fits. The person who was killed was in the same area a lot of these same victims were in. There were no witnesses, even though it was broad daylight. And the man suspected was described as a tall man with a scar through his right eyebrow. Raina said Damon has a scar through his right eyebrow."

"What?" Marcus breathed. "How did I not know that?"

Karli shrugged.

"Why does that matter?" Cade asked Marcus. There was more going on than any of them knew, but something spooked Marcus.

Marcus met Cade's gaze. "This case... It was tied to another one. A woman was murdered in an alley. Her throat was cut after they beat her. The man killed was one of the two men who beat and killed the woman."

"Sounds like the world is better without him in it," Karli said.

Marcus nodded. "I agree, but there were two witnesses

to that woman's death. One wasn't reliable, but the other faced a man with a scar over his right eyebrow. He almost killed her. He would have, too."

"You seem to know a lot about this case. I don't remember reading about that one," Karli said.

"You won't because it's not public record. But the witness, the one who was almost killed, was Frannie."

"What?" Karli gasped.

Marcus nodded.

"Who's Frannie?" Cade asked.

Marcus looked at him. "My wife. She's never forgiven herself for not stopping him from killing that woman, but if you're right and *Eyebrow* from almost twenty years ago is Damon Street, Frannie will blame herself for all of this. Because she had him, but he got away."

"Oh, my God," Karli breathed.

DAMON KICKED the gravel on the sidewalk and looked up and down the dark street. He fucking hated waiting. He had more important things to do than stand around and wait for someone else to show up. But he had no choice. If he wanted to keep his position in the Company, and not end up in a ditch somewhere, he had to wait.

A vehicle finally turned the corner. The headlights shined brightly, illuminating the otherwise inky black night. The SUV crawled toward Damon, the driver not in a hurry.

He finally stopped next to where Damon waited. He parked the vehicle and got out, his body cam still in the vehicle with his gun and the other cameras that monitored every movement of a police officer on duty.

"I got a call," Officer Bernard said. "A neighbor reported seeing a man loitering in this area."

"What else is the neighbor going to report?" Damon snarled.

Bernard was a cocky son-of-a-bitch. He thought he was untouchable by everyone. As a cop, civilians were scared of him. Or at least respected the badge and the rights it afforded him. Bernard was as dirty as they came, though. A cop for nearly twenty years, he'd been in Damon's pocket for most of his career. He'd taken out more witnesses than most of the people in the Company, but his job was to be invisible.

Bernard studied Damon and sucked his teeth. "It's not safe to meet, you know."

Damon nodded. "I've been given new orders."

"What kind of orders?" Bernard asked.

"The kind that say you're done."

Bernard raised one blond eyebrow and smirked. "And you think you're going to just kill me and walk away?"

"Orders are orders."

"You're going to listen to the boss now?" Bernard smirked.

He knew how Damon felt about the boss. Damon made the mistake of running his mouth a year or so ago about how he should have been the one chosen. Bernard had been holding that rant over his head since.

"It's just business."

"Who did the boss send to tell you to come after me?"

Damon scowled. How the fuck did Bernard know Damon had been knocked down? That the boss didn't even bother to call Damon personally but had sent Trevor to do it.

"So, the Golden Boy has lost his shine. I knew it was

going to happen when that bitch got away from you. You never should have let her live."

"I didn't fucking tell her to go!" Damon shouted.

Bernard raised a brow again. "Be careful. Someone might report another disturbance. Then you wouldn't get to find out the information I learned today."

"What information?"

Bernard tsked. "See, if I tell you, then I lose my leverage. I did you a favor killing that stupid slime ball. You made a mistake hiring him to get to your ex. He would have sold you out in a heartbeat if he thought it would get him free. In fact, he did. He told me everything."

"What the hell does that have to do with anything?" Damon demanded. He was getting more than a little sick of Bernard's games.

"It means the recording I took of our conversation just might end up in the *right* hands if something happens to me."

"You'll go down as an accomplice. Covering it up and killing the guy."

Bernard shrugged. "If I'm dead, what do I care?"

Damon growled and pulled his gun from his waistband. He pointed it at the other man's jaw and snarled. "What the fuck do you think you know? Tell me so I can kill you."

Bernard chuckled. "You think you're so smart. You're going to pull a gun on me and I'm just going to sing my song to you. Why would I do that?"

"Fine. Then how about you tell me and I'll let you go," Damon suggested. He let go of Bernard and shoved his gun back into his waistband.

Bernard shrugged. "You'll be stuck here for a little while anyway. But while you're... resting, you can think about how you hired some dumb fuck to kill someone, and he killed the wrong woman."

"What?" Damon barked. His head felt funny. Like he was off-balance.

Bernard grinned. "Your superstar smashed in the head of the wrong woman. Karli Sloane is still alive."

"You're wrong."

Bernard shook his head. "I could be, but I don't think I am. After Jessica German was released, our captain has been having a lot of secret meetings. The one he went to today was with a woman who looked a hell of a lot like Karli Sloane. Which makes me wonder who's in her grave?"

Damon stumbled, trying to make sense of Bernard's words and trying to figure out why he couldn't stand up straight.

"Have a good nap, Damon. You'll be okay in about ten minutes. Enough time for me to make sure I could get away from here if you actually did try to kill me."

"Fuck you," Damon slurred.

"Always a pleasure, sir," Bernard snarled. Then he walked around his vehicle and got in. He drove off, leaving Damon slumped over on the sidewalk in his own piss without a person in the world knowing where he was.

10

KARLI BARELY REMEMBERED THE REST OF THE DAY. WHEN Marcus said Frannie might have encountered Damon years ago, and that he almost killed her, Karli felt like she'd been kicked in the gut. One man who was tied to all of them. One man who caused so much havoc.

Her heart ached for Tonya and Edie. For the hell she was sure Edie was going through, or had been through. Tonya was strong for not backing down. For being willing to stand up and say something wasn't right and that her cousin deserved better than to be forgotten. Too many people, especially women who looked like them, were forgotten. Never a second thought.

Karli was not going to let it happen to Edie.

After Marcus left, Karli and Cade worked in quiet companionship. They moved together through the rest of the day, as though neither could stand to be far from the other or say anything to make the new truth about their situation any less horrible.

Cade ordered dinner on the way to his apartment and didn't have to ask Karli to walk in with him. She was out of the SUV and on the sidewalk waiting for him when he got there. He took her hand and held her close when they went inside and again as they returned to the vehicle. He did the same when they walked up to his apartment, then locked the door behind them and double checked it couldn't be opened easily.

Karli stared at the pizza in the box and tried to talk herself into eating a slice. She was hungry, but after the day they'd had, she wasn't sure she could stomach eating.

"If you want to go somewhere else, I understand," Cade said quietly. He was standing behind her, still close to the door. He hadn't left the entryway since they got back to his place.

"What are you talking about? Go where? Why would I want to go somewhere else?" Karli turned to look at him.

He ran a hand over his hair. His gaze was vacant. Wounded. Regretful. "I never should have taken Tonya's case. I knew it was a bad idea, but I wanted a chance to be a hero."

"You don't anymore?"

Cade shook his head slowly. "I'm not a hero. I never should have tried to pretend I could be."

He dug into his pocket and walked toward her. For half a second, Karli wondered if he was going to hurt her, if he had a weapon. Then she saw his phone.

"I'm going to take a shower. Use this to call whoever you need to call. I know you're not using Tonya's phone, but you can use mine. You're better off nowhere near this whole thing."

"Are you giving up?"

Cade met her gaze. His was hard. Furious. Determined. "Never. But I'd never forgive myself if you were killed because of me. I can drop you off somewhere or someone can come get you while I'm in the shower. It's up to you."

"Cade," Karli tried, but he walked away and didn't look back.

Karli stared at his phone. He'd unlocked it before handing it to her. She could call anyone. But her reality was she didn't want to.

When Tonya walked into her apartment, Karli reacted. She panicked and left, and Tonya died. If Karli had stayed, there was no guarantee anything would have been different, but she'd forever live with the guilt that she walked away and another woman died in her place.

She'd never been so scared in her life. At the moment, she had no idea if she would survive if Tonya had found her. She didn't know who Tonya was or why she was there, so Karli left. She took off. She fled... like a coward.

No more.

She refused to let Damon or Silver or anyone else take anything from her again. Tonya was the least threatening of all of them, but Karli didn't know that at the time. Running saved her life, but she couldn't live with herself if she didn't do everything possible to make sure Damon never hurt anyone else again.

She had to do it for Tonya. For Edie. For Raina.

Raina lived with the bastard. She loved him. She gave herself to him. And he nearly killed her for it. He would have if she hadn't escaped him when she did. She wouldn't be safe until Damon was gone. Dead or in jail, it didn't matter, but stripped of his network and no longer in power.

Karli's throat tightened with fear. Fighting back could cost Karli her life. Stopping Damon wouldn't be simple. But walking away after everything she knew, after the murders and the victims and the innocent lives Damon took, was not a fucking option.

Karli had to be better. She had to fight back. She had to...

The bathroom door opened, and all thought stopped except fucking hell, Cade was a work of art.

He stepped out in just a towel. Water dripped from the ends of his hair onto his shoulders and raced over the sculpted muscles of his chest.

Adrenaline coursed through Karli's body. Fear mixed with desire was a dangerous combination. One she wasn't sure she could fight.

"I forgot to grab clothes," Cade said, taking a step toward her instead of going toward the bedroom.

Karli's gaze drifted to his towel, where a bulge swelled in the front. She licked her lips, the slick of her tongue the first she realized what she did.

"Karli," Cade groaned. He moved closer still. The towel tented more.

Karli faced him and took a step toward him.

"Did you call anyone?" he asked, nodding to the dark phone on the table next to the pizza box.

She shook her head. "There's nowhere I'd rather be."

"It's dangerous," Cade said.

"So's letting a man like Damon walk free. I can't do it. Raina will never be safe. Tonya will have died for nothing. Edie... I can't even imagine what she's going through."

"This isn't your fight."

"You said you're not giving up. Why should I? He sent someone to kill me. Someone who would have done exactly that if Tonya hadn't been there at the same time. She died for me, even though it wasn't intentional. I can't walk away."

"From the case."

Karli's gaze followed a single drop of water that nestled in the dark hair on his chest. It fought the tangled web and splintered off in different directions before it was absorbed by his skin. All Karli could think was she wanted to lick that same path.

"You can't look at me like that," Cade hissed.

"I can't stop."

"Fuck." Cade snarled and took the last few steps between them. His hand speared into her hair, tilting her head as he lowered his mouth to hers and claimed her all at once.

Karli whimpered, then moaned when his tongue parted her lips and found hers. She lifted her hands, splaying them wide on his chest and delighting in the soft hair covering it.

His skin was warm and damp. His muscles were firm and twitched under her fingertips. His kiss was relentless, a battle with her as much as with himself. She felt his resistance, the way he held himself back from overpowering her and sought to snap that control and have all of him.

Even if it was just for a night.

"Is this what you want?" Cade whispered against her ear. "Because if you don't want me inside you, I need to know."

"I want you inside me," Karli whispered back.

His breath heaved from him, his chest rising and falling with each force of air. His hands tugged at her hair before sliding out of her curls and finding her hips. He pulled her in tight, letting her feel the thickness of his erection between them.

"I need you to be sure, Karli. Before I take you to my room, I need you to be sure. I've been dying to see you stretched out on my bed, but I'll stop now if that's what you want."

"I want you inside me, Cade. Now."

He groaned at her words and wrapped his arms so tight around her she could barely breathe. He walked them toward the bedroom, half carrying her as he moved.

"You're so fucking beautiful," he whispered as he trailed his lips down her neck to the collar of her shirt. "So beautiful."

She wasn't sure he meant it, but she wasn't going to question it. Her life was not in a place where she could think farther ahead than the moment. She wasn't ready for a relationship, and they weren't starting one. He was protecting her. He was keeping her safe. And they were working together to bring down one of the worst criminals Karli had ever heard of.

Tonight, this moment, it was all about blowing off steam and letting out the adrenaline that pulsed through them. It didn't mean more than any other one-night stand. Even if they would be waking up and spending the foreseeable future together.

Cade lifted the edge of her shirt. He kissed the exposed skin, giving her time to get used to him seeing her naked. When his lips reached the underside of her bra, he licked the flesh that settled beneath the edge of the always too small cup.

Karli reached back and unhooked her bra, hating that he was getting an up-close-and-personal view of what it was like to have boobs that were too big for most bras. Her breasts bounced free, settling on her plump belly as she lifted the bra out of the way.

"Perfect," Cade moaned, cupping one and raising it to his lips. He licked around her nipple, then closed his teeth over the peak.

Karli gasped at the jolt that ran through her. He smiled against her breast, then moved to the other one and did the same. Karli held him to her, wanting him to never stop.

His fingers brushed her belly, sliding beneath the waistband of her pants. She let go of his head and fought to pull her shirt and bra off.

"You're distracting me," Cade growled when she was fully topless. "I can't resist these breasts." He cupped them again, bringing them to his mouth together and sucking hard on both nipples. He licked them and teased them until Karli was moaning and her eyes rolled back in her head.

Cade moved them to the bed and eased her down while he continued to toy with her nipples. With her back on the mattress, he kissed his way down her body, circling her belly button with his tongue before hooking his fingers into her waistband and easing her pants and panties down and off her legs.

"Jesus, you're stunning. I am a lucky man."

Karli let the compliment roll around inside her. The evil bitch in her head said not to believe him, but Karli told her to sit down and shut up and enjoy the orgasms she was sure Cade would deliver.

Cade started at her knees and licked the inside of her thighs. He kissed his way back down, ramping up her desire with every brush of his lips and tongue on her body. When he blew his warm breath over her soaked flesh, she moaned and squirmed and was rewarded with his tongue on her clit.

"Oh, God," Karli whispered.

Cade licked her clit lazily. Like an ice cream cone on a cold day, he took his time, in no rush to hurry to the end of the treat. Karli was desperate for a little more urgency and grunted when he didn't move things along.

"What do you want, Karli?" he asked, nipping the inside of her thigh, then soothing the sting with his tongue.

"I want to come," she snapped.

"On my tongue?"

"Yes."

"How about on my fingers?"

"Please."

"What about with my cock stretching you wide open? Where I can watch as I disappear inside you?"

"Cade."

"All of the above?"

"Yes," she shouted as he sucked on her clit and sent her flying in an instant.

"More," he demanded, not giving up as she soared high. He pressed two thick fingers into her and pulled her clit into his mouth, capturing the nub between his tongue and the roof of his mouth.

Karli stayed high, moaning his name as her body rode wave after wave of an orgasm so powerful she wasn't sure she could think straight ever again.

The next thing she knew, he was tearing a foil wrapper. "Look at me, beautiful."

Karli blinked her eyes open, wondering how long she was spaced out with orgasmic bliss.

"I love those eyes," he said. "Are you ready for me?"

She nodded and moaned when he eased his way into her. She expected him to thrust in all at once, but no, he surprised her again by taking his time.

"So tight," he groaned. "You feel so fucking good."

Karli clenched around him when he was fully seated, and they both moaned.

"Fuck, Karli."

The edges of his control started to slip, giving her a glimpse of the man he was trying to hold back. The man she desperately wanted to know.

Cade pulled out, then slid back in slowly. The friction it created between them was enough for Karli to tremble. She'd dated plenty of men who were at least as big as him, but she'd never been with a man who liked to take things slow.

She was starting to think she might be a fan.

"Cade," she breathed.

"More?"

She nodded, biting her lip as her channel tightened around him. The slow, steady strokes were enough to send her up again, and the occasional slam deep inside hit just right.

"I can't wait to feel you come on my dick." Cade leaned over her, changing the angle he entered, and Karli moaned low in her throat. "That sounded good."

Karli nodded, unable to form a concrete thought, let alone words. The nest of hair around his cock rubbed her clit with each stroke in, adding fuel to the fire he was building inside her. It wasn't long before Karli was panting for breath and begging for release.

And Cade was more than capable of getting her there.

"You're so beautiful," he grunted. "These breasts bouncing every time I slam into you is making me want to come. I'm so fucking close, Karli."

"Me, too," she breathed.

He grabbed one breast and squeezed it. He rubbed his thumb over her nipple and lifted it to his mouth. The second her nipple went into his mouth, her entire body let go and she came with a shout.

"Oh, fuck," Cade growled. Her release set off a beast in him, one that didn't hold back and didn't listen to the man who tried to maintain control.

He pounded into her ruthlessly, his strokes shaking the

entire bed. Karli moaned with him, mesmerized as his face twisted with pleasure at his impending orgasm. He gritted his teeth, then tensed every muscle in his body before roaring through his orgasm while he twitched and trembled deep inside her.

Karli had never seen anything so beautiful in her life. A man like him, one who never let his guard down, giving her just a tiny peek into who he was when he wasn't so strict. A man who lost himself fully inside her and collapsed onto her without a thought to anything other than his inability to do more than lie there and struggle to breathe.

It was amazing.

Karli let her hands run up and down his sweaty back. She wanted to remember the way he smelled and the way he looked and the way he sounded forever. If she survived what they were doing, bringing down Damon, she wanted to remember the night they shared. Cade wouldn't be hers forever, but for the moment, she was the one he'd buried himself in and let go of the weight of the world for. He allowed her to forget the horrors they read about that day for a little while, and she hoped she'd done the same for him.

And until tomorrow, she hoped they could stay in their bubble and not think about what they were facing.

Cade pushed off her a minute later, getting off the bed and leaving the room. The water ran as he washed his hands, then he was back in the doorway with a smile and nothing else on.

"I don't know about you, but I need some food before I join you in this bed again."

"You're going to join me again?" Karli asked, surprised he was interested in round two.

He pushed off from the doorframe. His smile faded. "I don't have to. I shouldn't have said that."

Karli scrambled off the bed and stepped on his towel as he reached down to pick it up.

He looked up at her.

She crossed her arms and raised one brow at him.

He mimicked her stance.

"I'd much prefer you leave it there."

His cock twitched. "Why is that?"

"I was surprised. I know this is just... I don't know... but I figured you got me out of your system."

He shook his head. "Not even close. Did you get me out of yours?"

"Nope."

"Good. Then pizza? And bed?"

Karli nodded. "I like the way you think."

"I like the way you fuck." Cade slapped her gently on the ass, then turned and led the way to the living room.

Karli was right behind him.

11

———

Cade was awake long before the sun was up. Long before Karli stirred beside him. He couldn't stop the smile that lifted his lips or the thoughts that lifted his cock.

It had been a long time since he spent time with a woman who made him feel like he didn't have to change everything about himself in order to be worthy of her. Karli was unapologetically herself, and she made him feel like he could be the same.

Starting with trusting his instincts.

Cade eased out of bed, not wanting to leave the warm woman behind, but knowing he had work to do. Normally, he'd spend half his work hours in the office and half on the road looking for someone or following them. Without knowing where Damon could be, or where Edie was, Cade had to do a lot more digging.

But Karli had done a lot of it for him.

He grabbed a pair of shorts on his way out of the bedroom and softly closed the door. He stepped into the shorts and tiptoed across the apartment to the living room. He turned on the lamp next to the couch, then grabbed his computer and notepad. He always took notes when he was working on cases. It helped him piece things together.

Karli shared her notes on the cases she looked into, and Cade combined the two lists they had. Most of their cases overlapped, but there were a few they each had independent of the other. Those were the cases Cade needed to look into.

He re-read the police files on the cases Karli pulled, the ones he'd dismissed. He tried to see what she might have picked up on, her notes an added bonus.

She was untrained, but sometimes that was an advantage. She saw things he didn't, and connected things in a different way. When he got to the second case she flagged, he stopped.

Karli noted a case from a decade ago. It was a woman who moved to the area in her early twenties. She worked a few different jobs before she disappeared one night when she was supposed to meet friends for drinks.

Cade dismissed it as nothing when he saw it because it didn't seem like anything out of the ordinary or special. The woman was never found, but there was also no evidence of foul play.

Karli's notes had *Edie?* in a circle. He hadn't picked up on the similarities before. Maybe because it had been so long, or maybe because he was looking for more concrete evidence, but either way, she was right. It sounded exactly how Tonya described Edie's case when she pled with him to help her find her cousin.

Cade flipped through the rest of the cases, adding his notes to Karli's until he had a list he thought was fairly comprehensive. It was hard to imagine one man could inflict such trauma in a city, but Damon Street didn't have his reputation for being a good samaritan.

Karli underlined street names in some of her cases, and when Cade went back and looked, he realized a lot of them happened within a few miles of each other. Similar to Marcus's wife's case, the proximity of all the incidents was something of interest. If Damon spent most of his time in that location, they could find him.

Cade was buried so deep in his research and plotting all the cases that he didn't notice Karli until she ran a hand over his bare back. He jumped, and she backed away quickly.

"Sorry. I thought you heard me coming."

Cade shook his head. "I was focused. Sorry."

"It's okay." Karli wrapped her arms around her middle and gave him a tight smile.

Cade set the computer on the coffee table and stood. He moved around the couch toward her, feeling better when she didn't back away from him. "I didn't mean to scare you."

Karli nodded and let him pull her into his arms. "It's okay. I was surprised when I woke up and you weren't there. I figured…"

Cade got it. "I left you there. Shit. No. I just couldn't sleep. I kept thinking about the cases we went over yesterday and wanted to take another look at things."

"Did you figure out anything else?"

"Besides Damon Street is an evil bastard who doesn't deserve to live."

"Yeah, since we already knew that."

Cade breathed a laugh and went back to his notes. He flipped to the last page where he'd been taking his latest notes. "I think you were onto something with the locations. There are a few that are outside his normal space, but so many incidents are close that it's hard to imagine he doesn't have an office, for lack of a better word, somewhere in the warehouse district."

"I was thinking that, too. We should go there today and look around. Maybe see if any companies around there have cameras we can see the footage from."

"Most companies don't like giving civilians their security footage."

"We don't need most. We just need one."

Cade laughed and shook his head. "Ever the optimist."

"I'm not so sure about that, but I'm not willing to give up. I want my life back."

"Is it so bad being here?" Cade asked. He didn't like her being in danger, but he was starting to get used to having her around. It was far less lonely than things had been since Alanna.

"No, but I had a life before all of this. Friends and family. My job."

"I'm sorry. I didn't really think about it. This has to be hard for you."

Karli nodded. "It feels like all of this is happening to someone else. Like I'm not really living my life, you know?"

Cade shook his head. "Not really. But I get being thrown for a loop and feeling like nothing is what you thought it was."

"Yeah, that's basically it. All of this started because Tonya broke into my apartment looking for information about her cousin. She had no idea it would get her killed or that she would set off this chain of events."

"She would have given her life for her cousin. Edie was the only family Tonya had left. She said they grew up together and were like sisters."

"I have a cousin like that," Karli said softly.

"Have you been in touch with her?"

Karli shook her head. "She has an important job. And I don't want to risk her getting hurt by reaching out."

"But you risked it to see your friends."

"They're local. I didn't have to make a phone call. It was different."

"You called me," Cade said.

Karli grinned. "I was willing to risk that. I didn't know if I could trust you."

Cade laughed. "So I was expendable?"

"Pretty much, yeah."

Cade gasped in mock anger and prowled toward her. "I think you deserve to be punished for that."

"Oh, yeah?"

"Absolutely. Only one orgasm this time. Not three."

"That is torture," Karli teased.

Cade caught her around the waist and wrapped his arms tight around her. "You shouldn't have said I was expendable."

"I didn't mean it," Karli said. She reached up and framed his face with her hands.

"Maybe you can get two."

"Deal," Karli agree before lifting on her toes to kiss him.

FOUR SCREAMING orgasms for her and one brain-melting one for him, and they were finally ready to leave for the day. As ready as they could be when they were going to be stalking a professional murderer.

Cade stayed close to Karli on the walk to his SUV. He looked around the parking lot for any vehicles that weren't normal or anyone lingering. He had his gun strapped to his ankle and hoped not to need it, but he wasn't taking any chances.

Cade's expectations for the day were low. They were going to drive around and hope someone would help them. Karli almost seemed to be enjoying the idea of doing something instead of just research.

"We can pretend to be lost or something," she suggested.

"Why would we need their surveillance videos?"

"Ooh, maybe our dog wandered off and someone said they spotted a dog that looked like ours nearby and we want to see if their cameras picked it up."

"That's a better one, but if the dog isn't there, what difference does it make if it's on the video?"

"Maybe we can see where the dog was going. It could be hurt, you know." She huffed and crossed her arms over her chest.

"The dog is fictional, Karli."

A laugh burst from her. "I forgot that part. Well, what do you think we should do?"

"I think we should look around for any buildings with cameras. If we find one, we can let Marcus know and he can get a warrant. Do things the legal way so Damon doesn't have a chance of getting away with anything on a technicality."

Karli pouted. "You're no fun. I wanted to pretend to be someone."

"Maybe one day," Cade said, smiling at her.

They drove through the area slowly. Most of the buildings were large warehouses with tall, flat exteriors. No windows, few doors, and only the occasional parking area.

Karli took notes on the addresses that had cameras. As Cade expected, it wasn't more than a handful. Most of them were in the parking lots, likely used to ensure employee safety. Stop signs were on most corners, eliminating the chances of traffic cameras, too.

Cade made the turn onto the last street they planned to drive down and eased his way past building after building. A dark SUV turned onto the street at the other end. Cade watched as the vehicle drew closer to them.

It was fancy. Large and black and out of place in the area. Between the work that happened there and the unpaved nature of many of the roads, the shiny, black vehicle stood out.

They were almost to the vehicle. Cade stared through the windshield at the driver, a man with a shaved head and shoulders that covered the entire seat he was in. He wore sunglasses and stared straight ahead, not even glancing toward Cade and Karli as they drove by.

When they passed each other, the SUV turned into a roll-up door and disappeared.

"Did you see that vehicle?" Cade asked Karli.

"Yeah, why?"

"Did it seem out of place to you?"

"I guess, but it could have been the owner of the company or something."

"Or it could have been Damon."

Karli shook her head. "I don't think Damon is as big as that guy. He looked like a tank."

Cade nodded and watched his rearview mirror to see if there was any motion at the building. "What if he was Damon's driver? Or bodyguard?"

Karli leaned back in her seat, then turned and looked back. "I didn't think about that. I just dismissed the guy because he didn't fit the description we have of Damon. What was the address?"

"I don't know, but I don't think we can drive back down the street without someone noticing."

"Crap."

"We also can't have Marcus get a warrant for the place without a reason."

"They're shady as fuck. That's the reason."

Cade snorted a laugh. "And this is why our justice system is messed up. Shady as fuck isn't enough. It would be nice if it was sometimes, though."

"No kidding."

"Where did Raina live when she lived with Damon?"

"It's empty. The cops searched it months ago. When she went to the shelter the way she was, they had enough to file charges on him for attempted murder. They went to get him, and the place looked like it had been vacant for months. It really scared Raina."

"That he cleared out so fast?"

"That and that he made it look like no one ever lived there. She said she had a really hard time with it. Marcus showed her pictures they took. It was completely empty. All her stuff was gone, but so was any sign anyone had been there in a long time. There was dust on the flat surfaces and everything."

"Seriously? That's some commitment."

"Yeah. It was unbelievable."

"And she's sure they went to the right place?"

"She told them where it was."

"Sure, but if it was an apartment building or something, he could have switched the numbers on the units or paid the building manager to give the police incorrect information."

"It was a penthouse apartment. Only one unit on the floor. There was no way for them to go to the wrong one."

"Wow. That's disturbing on a whole new level. But can you imagine if, after all this we've read about, he was taken down for domestic violence?"

"If he's in custody, they can charge him with other things. They just have to find him."

"True."

Cade drove around a little longer, then went to the office for the afternoon. They decided to cook dinner together and ordered groceries to pick up on the way to his apartment.

Karli was chopping carrots, and Cade was adding chicken to the marinade. She stopped for a minute and looked at him.

"What?" he asked.

"How are you able to spend all your time working on Tonya's case?"

Cade sucked in a breath. He busied himself with what he was doing and tried to decide if he wanted her to know the truth. If he told her, she might look at him differently. Like a man who couldn't keep his girlfriend happy. A man who focused too much on work to be around.

But lying to her didn't feel right either. They were working together and sleeping together and when one ended, the other might, too, but she still deserved the truth.

"I told you most of my cases were cheating spouses. They're usually easy cases, quick money. The cheater isn't usually as careful as they think they are. Especially since they have no idea who I am and don't bother to hide their actions when I'm following them. I hate cases like that, but they're good for paying the bills. I've also had worker's comp cases, a few fraud cases, mostly nonviolent crime type of stuff. I'm hired by the individual to look into whoever they feel wronged them."

"Okay," Karli said, drying her hands on a towel and focusing on him entirely.

Cade sighed. "I had an infidelity case. The couple had a lot of money and the wife was convinced the husband was sleeping with someone else. She'd hired other PIs, but none of them were able to find any evidence. She came to me. He was the one asking for a divorce, and he didn't want to give her much of anything. She came into the marriage with family money, and he used most of it to build a successful business. He wanted to leave her with nothing."

"Asshole," Karli muttered.

Cade smiled. "That's why I agreed to look into it. She would have gotten half their assets, but the company was a corporation and since she wasn't on the board, she wouldn't have access to any future profits. He filed for divorce, stating irreconcilable differences. With no fault on either side, the court would usually split things up and move on."

"Which would leave him with an entire company that she paid to build but had no legal right to."

"Exactly. If she could find proof he was cheating, she could refile with that as part of it and bring everything into the light about the company. It would give her lawyers access to more information about the company and everything."

"Okay, so you found the proof?"

Cade smiled at her confidence in him. He had the same once upon a time. He knew when Mrs. Waters walked into his office that he would be able to find out what was going on. He didn't know just how much he would find out, though.

"She told me his routine. I followed him at a distance for a while, confirming where he went and what was normal for him. I couldn't get into his office or home, but I could see where he was going and who he was talking to."

"And?"

Cade sucked in a breath. "I found him with another woman. I followed him one afternoon after he went to the gym. He drove to her house and let himself in with a key he had."

Cade was quiet for a long moment as the scene replayed in his mind. He didn't realize how long he stood there silently until Karli put a hand on his arm and said his name.

"Sorry." He forced a smile for her. "Anyway, they were in her bedroom at the back of the house. She was screaming his name as he pounded into her from behind."

"That's detailed. It sounds like you were in the room."

"I was."

"What? You broke into her house?"

He laughed mirthlessly. "Nope. I had a key. Because she was my girlfriend at the time."

12

"Holy shit," Karli breathed. She leaned back against the cabinet and tried to wrap her head around what he was telling her.

"Yeah." Cade ran his hand over his head. "Obviously, I ended things with her, but to make things worse, the husband claimed the affair was entrapment. He said his wife orchestrated the entire thing so she could get access to his company. Since there was a documented history between myself and Alanna, and Mrs. Waters hired me, the judge sided with the husband and my client lost her case."

"Fuck."

"And then she dragged my name through the mud. She never said anything that wasn't true, so I couldn't sue her for slander, but it ruined my career. No one wanted to hire me for infidelity cases anymore. And before long, no one wanted to hire me for any cases."

"Wow. That's a mess."

Cade nodded. "Yep. So, when Tonya showed up, she was desperate. She had already gone to other PIs, and no one wanted to go after Damon Street. She was about to give up, but I had nothing else going on and I'd gone through almost all of my savings, so I agreed to take her case. I needed the money in order to keep my company open. Of course now, I'm not sure what's going to happen."

"Did she pay you?"

Cade nodded. "Half upfront, and she was supposed to pay expenses. Right now, I feel I owe her. She just wanted to find her cousin."

"You're a good man, Cade Murray."

He snorted. "Just not a smart one. My girlfriend was cheating on me, and I had no clue."

"You had no clue? Really?"

"Do you think I should have known something?" he snapped.

Karli shook her head and stepped toward him. "No. But I'm surprised. You don't seem to miss much. You are able to see things others wouldn't. You really had no idea your ex was cheating on you?"

Cade blew out a heavy breath. "I didn't have any proof."

"But you had a suspicion."

"That makes it sound like I knew and ignored it."

"I think it sounds like you didn't want to get hurt. My friend, Jessica, was in love with Braden for years. She worked for his sister, and she would just fall all over herself when Braden was around. Whenever we'd talk about him, I'd tell her she should ask him to dinner or out for a drink or something, but she never would. She told me one time she'd rather tell herself he's too busy to notice her than know he's just not interested."

"Ouch. Is this the Jessica from the news?"

"Yes. She was at my apartment that day to tell me how her date with Braden had gone the night before."

"She took the leap?"

Karli shook her head. "No. He asked her out. His sister kind of talked him into it. Jessica wasn't really looking forward to the date because she knew he only did it to make his sister stop pushing him, but they're together now. Their date was really good, and he found her when she was in hiding and helped her. He risked everything for her, and now they're living together and working together."

"It sounds like that all worked out."

"It did. And it sounds like things with you and Alanna worked out, too. You found out who she really was. Before you got married or moved in together or had kids or anything."

"We never talked about any of that," Cade said firmly.

"Why not?"

"Because I didn't trust her a bit," he admitted. He breathed a laugh. "Shit. I guess I did know. On some level."

"And you would have figured it out, eventually. When you were ready to face it."

"Maybe."

"Definitely," Karli said. She stepped forward until they were toe-to-toe. "You deserve better than someone who doesn't see how amazing you are."

His lips turned up in a ghost of a smile, one tainted with pain and distrust. "I'm still not sure about that, but thank you."

"I am. We might not know each other well, but I know enough about you to know you're a good man. You should have someone in your life that sees that and returns it. You deserve better."

"Thank you." He stepped forward and kissed her gently, pulling her into his arms. His tongue licked the seam of her lips, silently asking for entry.

Karli parted her lips to welcome him in, wrapping her

arms around his waist. He was one of the good ones. A man every woman wanted for her own. How any woman could be dumb enough to have him and throw him away for a cheater was beyond comprehensible.

Karli was not going to make the same mistake. She was going to enjoy every moment she had with Cade, no matter how long it lasted.

Their kiss wasn't rushed or impatient. He kissed her like there was nothing stopping him from staying in that spot all night.

Karli couldn't remember the last time she kissed a man without knowing it was going to lead to sex. Cade made no move to guide her to the bedroom or to touch her anywhere else. He just kissed her like he couldn't get enough of kissing her.

Which was completely fine with her.

He finally gentled the kiss and started to pull back. He dove back in once more, smiling against her lips when she laughed in surprise. "I really like kissing you."

"Me, too."

"Thank you for not laughing at me when I told you about Alanna."

"Why in the world would I have laughed at you?"

"You have no idea how many people did."

"Well, they're shitty. You did nothing wrong. She's the one who was dating you and slept with someone else. That's not on you."

"Yeah, but—"

"No. Hell no. I don't care if you refused sex for a year, or worked twenty-four-seven. If you were in a relationship, she had no right to cheat. And if she wasn't happy in the rela-tionship, she should have ended it. There's never an excuse for cheating and the person who was cheated on does not hold all the blame. I don't know what happened between the two of you, but she still made the choice she made and you took the fall for it in your career. That doesn't make it your fault. Ever."

"Thank you," Cade whispered.

Karli leaned against his chest and held him close. They stood there together for a minute, just holding each other.

She didn't know who moved first, but when they broke apart, she went back to cutting up carrots and he turned on the news.

"A body was found on Morgan Avenue earlier tonight. The woman has not been identified. Police are looking for anyone with any information or anyone who may have been in the area between eleven and three today."

"That's where we were," Karli breathed.

"I know," Cade said. He already had his phone out. "I'm calling Captain Patrick."

"Why?"

"Because we were there. And I'd rather have it known we were driving around instead of have someone tell him and it come back on us and we look like suspects."

"Shit. I never thought of that," Karli said.

Cade spoke to Marcus and told him about their drive-by investigation. From Cade's side of the conversation, Marcus wasn't too thrilled. Cade told him about the vehicle they drove by and where it turned in, and relayed the addresses they'd pulled together of all the buildings that appeared to have surveillance.

Karli started cooking while Cade talked to Marcus. She needed to do something mindless so she could forget for just a minute that they could have driven right past someone being killed. They could have been there.

Was it Damon?

The question echoed in her mind constantly. She couldn't ignore it and say no. They were in the area because they believed he might be. Was he? And did he kill that woman?

"Marcus said they searched the warehouse we saw that SUV pull into," Cade said from behind her.

"And?"

"It was a regular old warehouse. But the body was found close to it, so they had cause to search there."

"Close or there?" Karli asked. She turned to face him, seeing the exhaustion and worry in the lines of his face.

"Technically, the body was in front of the warehouse, but it wasn't near a door. Marcus said it looked like she was dumped there."

"They don't know who she was."

Cade shook his head.

"Was it just a coincidence we were there today and a body shows up?"

"I don't know. All I know is we're getting closer."

"Closer to what? To getting ourselves killed? To unleashing more hell on this city? To coming face-to-face with one of the most dangerous men ever?" Karli screeched.

"Come here," Cade said soothingly as he pulled her in.

Karli fought the comfort. It was all too much. Tears broke free. She buried her face in Cade's shoulder and tried to stop the flow.

"It'll be okay," Cade whispered.

Karli shook her head. "Not for Tonya. Maybe not for Edie. Not for Raina. He's a monster. We have dozens of cases we think he was involved in, and God knows how many more there are out there. He kills without a thought and dumps bodies wherever he wants to. How do you stop someone like him? Someone who has no sense of morals or fear?"

"I don't know," Cade admitted. "I don't know."

Karli finally calmed down enough to eat dinner, then she took a shower and went to bed. Cade wasn't sure if she wanted him to join her or not, so he stayed on the couch.

He let the TV make noise as he tried to put the pieces of the case together. If it was just a missing person case, it would have been easier, but the case was so much bigger than just Edie. It was Tonya and Karli and Raina and Captain Patrick's wife and who knew how many more people who'd been killed or silenced or raped or harmed in some way.

Cade must have fallen asleep because the next thing he knew, Karli was curling up with him on the couch.

"Hey," he said, his voice rough with sleep.

"I thought you were going to come into the bedroom." She tugged the blanket off the back of the couch and wrapped it around her warm body, snuggling up close to him.

"I wasn't sure if you want me to."

"I did," she said softly.

"I'm sorry."

"For?"

"For not joining you. You were upset, and I thought you might want your space tonight."

She shook her head. "I wanted to feel like all of this isn't for nothing. To feel like we're going to stop him. Stop all of it."

"I wish I could tell you we will, but I don't know."

"I need to know something good is coming out of this."

"Like what?" he asked, his throat thick with desire. Her husky voice was going straight to his cock, and her warm body and the weight of her against him wasn't helping.

"You. Us. I'm not saying there has to be an us after all of this, but for right now, I need to know this is good."

"It is good, Karli. It's so good. You're good."

She lifted her head to look at him, a sleepy, sexy smile on her face. "So are you."

He leaned down and kissed her. Her lips were soft under his and parted as soon as they connected. She whimpered and flicked her tongue alongside his.

He groaned, hardening instantly. Her hand slid around his waist. She shifted as they kissed, moving closer to him, then lifting to her knees.

Cade shifted to give her space and guided her hips as she straddled his. She sank down onto him, her heat beckoning to him. He groaned and surged up against her, desperate for her all at once.

"I need you, Cade." She dragged her nails over his scalp and tugged at the short hairs on the back of his head.

He groaned in response and cupped her breast, teasing the perky nipple through the thin shirt she'd chosen to sleep in. Her shorts were just as thin, letting him feel her heat and catch her scent when she shifted her body to bring them closer together.

"Karli," he whispered.

She shifted again, rubbing herself along his length. Flames licked at his body, his control slipping as she used him for what she needed. Whatever she needed.

"Please," she begged him, rocking over his hips and bringing herself closer to an orgasm.

He wanted to see her fall apart almost as much as he

wanted to feel her fall apart. He lifted her shirt until he could get his mouth on one of her nipples. He slicked his tongue over it, then sucked it hard into his mouth.

Her hips sped up, her head thrown back as desire took over.

Cade met her strokes with his own, dry-fucking her into her first orgasm. She trembled and cried out, his lips around her nipple and his tongue flicking the tip as she came.

Before she could come all the way down from the small peak she took herself over, he eased his hand into the leg opening of her shorts. Her panties were soaked already, and her widespread thighs were open for his fingers to take advantage of.

He worked his way beneath the edge of her panties and pressed a finger inside her. She moaned and her hips rocked again.

Cade twisted his wrist for better access and shoved her panties to the side so he could press his thumb to her clit.

"Cade!" she cried.

"You're not done," he growled as her body rippled around his finger. He added a second finger, loving it when her body opened for him and sucked him in deep.

"Please." Her whispered word was barely loud enough for him to hear.

With his lips on her nipples and his hand between her thighs, Cade made her forget everything except his name. She quivered and bucked. She shouted and whimpered. She came with a shout, then sank against him and breathed heavily in his ear.

"That was amazing," she whispered.

"You're amazing," he said. It was cheesy, but it was true. She impressed him. She not only worked hard to figure out what was going on, but she knew what she needed to survive it. She wasn't turning to drugs or alcohol after all they'd seen and read. She went to him. She asked him for what she needed. An escape that wouldn't cause harm to anyone.

She smiled at him, her lips barely lifting with her exhaustion. She pushed off him and stood, slowly removing all her clothes while he sat there and enjoyed the best show he'd ever seen.

"You're so damn beautiful," he whispered.

She shook her head and looked away. "I don't usually think so."

"But?"

She shrugged. "You're making me brave. I've never been willing to have sex with the lights on."

"You should show off these curves. You're sexy as fuck, Karli."

Her lips lifted in a smile she tried to fight, but Cade wasn't having that.

He grabbed himself and stroked through his pants. "I can't get enough of you. I'm hard as hell right now after you rubbed yourself all over me and came so hard. I can barely think straight when you're around, and after being inside you, I want more. Always more."

She sucked in a breath and licked her lips. "I want to taste you."

"I want to fuck you."

"After. I want to know what you taste like."

"Jesus, that's sexy," he growled. Cade yanked off his shirt and surged to his feet, crowding her space. She didn't step back, just stayed right there, pressed against him while he unbuttoned his pants and shoved them down.

He sank onto the couch again and stroked himself. She

stepped back and lowered to her knees. "Do you have a condom?"

"In my wallet," he said.

"Get it now because when you tell me to stop, I want to climb on top of you."

"Fucking hell," he groaned. He grabbed for his wallet and flung his keys to the floor in his hurry. He dug out the condom and set it on the table next to the couch, not caring where his wallet landed when Karli dropped to her knees in front of him.

She leaned forward, her large breasts getting in the way. She pushed his thighs apart so her breasts could settle between them.

The tender flesh of her nipples brushed the inside of his thighs and they both groaned. Then she closed her mouth over his cock and Cade saw stars.

"Fucking hell," he hissed.

She sucked him in deep, using her nails on his thighs. The sharpness of it kept him focused on what she was doing instead of letting him lose himself in her.

And he wanted to focus. He didn't want to miss one fucking second of Karli's lips wrapped around his dick.

He surged up into her mouth, and she groaned and dug her nails in. He slid his hands into her hair and bit back the urge to fuck her mouth while she sucked on him.

"You feel so fucking good," he whispered. "I love seeing your lips around my cock."

She smiled at that.

"I'm gonna need you to stop soon, though. You feel too good."

She groaned, then sped up. She pumped him in and out, and when a hand dipped between her thighs, he nearly let go right there.

"Oh, fuck, Karli. Stop. I need to be inside you now."

He yanked her off him, pulsing as she kept touching herself while he rolled the condom down his length. Her strokes were lazy, light strokes over her clit, but when he helped her crawl onto the couch and guided her over his cock, she stopped.

"Let me see," he said.

"You can do it."

He shook his head. "I want to see what you like. How you like to come. I love that you trust me enough to do that in front of me."

She bit her lip. "You tasted really good. I didn't want to stop."

Cade slammed his hips up, sinking his cock deep inside her. She moaned, and her eyes fell closed.

"You feel good, Karli. So fucking good."

Her hand slid between them. He held her hips and moved their bodies, fucking her hard as her fingers plucked her clit and rubbed over it quickly.

He felt her body tighten on his and had to bite back his orgasm.

"I'm close," she whispered.

"Don't hold back. Let me feel you. I'm right there with you, Karli."

She moaned, and her fingers flew faster. She bounced with his efforts, shifting forward so he hit her in the right spot inside. Her breath puffed out in moans, her eyes closed.

He watched it all, his gaze flicking from her breasts to her fingers to her entrance to her face, then around again.

"Cade," she whispered.

"Now, Karli. Come now."

He slammed up into her, holding her hips and bouncing

her body on his. Her fingers pressed hard on her clit, her nails digging into the swollen nub.

And she let go. Her mouth fell open in a silent scream for half a second before the real one came out. Her body shook and bounced and twitched as she came harder than he'd seen yet.

He was so lost in watching her he didn't notice his orgasm was right there until his body ripped apart at the seams. He shouted her name, leaning forward to sink his teeth into her shoulder as he erupted.

She twitched around him and above him, her body warm and sweaty and perfect. Cade didn't want to move. He wanted to stay right there forever. He wanted to stay inside her and forget about everything except the way she smelled and the way she felt and the way she looked.

Nothing could be better than that. Nothing.

13

———

KARLI COULDN'T KEEP HER EYES OPEN. SEX THAT AMAZING wore her out and made her smile all the way into sleep.

She was still smiling when she woke up the next morning and Cade was in bed with her. He really was a beautiful man. And kind. His ex was a fool for cheating on him. Not because he was attractive but because he was good. After everything Karli had been through, between her career in LA and the hell she saw at work and now Damon, good was more and more important to Karli.

"Morning," Cade whispered.

"Sorry I woke you."

Cade shook his head and moved closer. His hand slithered around her hip and pulled her naked body to his. "Not sleeping."

Karli chuckled. He was snoring when her eyes opened.

"Fine. Not anymore." Cade kissed her arm and rested his head on her shoulder. "You smell good."

"I smell like sex."

"Damn good."

Karli wondered if there was a chance for a future

between them. She wasn't there yet, not totally, but she'd spent more time with him than the last dozen men she'd dated. Combined. Working and living together for almost a week was new for her. And she wasn't sure she hated it.

"I need to take a shower."

"I like the way you think."

"It wasn't meant to be an invitation," Karli said with a laugh.

"Are you saying I can't join you?"

His fingertips grazed her flesh, lifting goosebumps everywhere on her bare skin. She moaned softly when his hand danced over her thighs and brushed her clit.

"I can stop," he said, kissing his way up her arm.

"Don't you dare," she begged.

Cade smiled against her skin and nipped her plump breast. Then he was gone.

"What are you doing?"

"You said we needed to shower."

"Evil man."

"I'm bringing a condom."

"Smart man."

Cade chuckled as Karli jumped out of bed and raced to the shower ahead of him. His hands slid up and down her front as he pressed himself to her back. "I can't get enough of your body."

She tilted her head to the side for him to kiss a line down her neck. She stuck her hand under the water, more than ready for it to be warm enough for them to get in. As soon as it was, she pulled the curtain back and dragged him in with her.

The shower was small for two people, but Cade was efficient with his movements. He teased her with his fingers until she panted her way through an orgasm, then spun her to face the wall and bent her over. He entered her from behind, slamming hard enough into her that she splintered and came a second time. Her third orgasm raced through her with his as he pounded into her and encouraged her to touch herself like she did the night before.

Gone was the embarrassment and timidness. Karli needed to come, and she needed to come with Cade filling her.

As she came down from her third orgasm of the morning, Cade washed them both and turned off the water. He wrapped her in a towel and stepped out, leaving her to stand in the shower while he dried off and went through his morning routine in the bathroom.

It was weirdly familiar, even though they'd never shared this part of their day. Karli watched him as he ran his fingers through his short, dark hair and trimmed the edges of his beard. He hung up his towel and applied deodorant before winking at her and walking out of the bathroom completely naked.

Karli smiled to herself. It was very domestic. Something she'd never experienced before, but something that made her feel all warm and gooey inside.

She dried off and handled her morning routine before heading to the bedroom to get dressed. She ached to get some new clothes after wearing the same handful of things over and over again. She sighed as she put on her last clean pair of panties, again, and tugged the high school tee over her head. She slid her legs into her jeans and debated asking Cade for something to wear.

She shook her head at the thought. That was too much like something a girlfriend would do. She didn't know what they were, but she knew they weren't that. They were enjoying each other's company and making the most of the messed up situation they were tangled up in.

Cade already had coffee made and bacon out of the microwave when Karli joined him in the kitchen. She thanked him for making breakfast as he stirred their scrambled eggs in the pan.

"You can borrow something if you need to," he offered, sipping his coffee and watching her over the rim of the mug.

She instantly shook her head. "I'm good. I'll need to wash clothes again, though. If you don't mind."

"Of course not. I just thought you might want to change it up a bit and wear something else. It's okay if you don't."

"I've already invaded your home and work. I'm not sure you're going to be so kind if I invade your drawers."

"You can invade my drawers anytime you want," he said. He wrapped an arm around her and pulled her in for a quick, firm kiss that had her laughing.

"You know what I mean."

He chuckled. "I do. But you're welcome to anything in there if you need something to wear. Anytime."

Karli nodded and tried not to smile. Maybe there was a chance at something after their hell was behind them.

KARLI HAD BEEN LOOKING FORWARD to a quiet day at Cade's apartment. Sunday was always her day off from work, a day she could relax and be lazy. But Cade said he had to go to his office. He wanted to see if there was any new information about the woman who was killed the day before. Karli had almost forgotten about her. About how close they'd been to where she'd been killed.

Reality was a sharp slap to the face.

They didn't rush to get to the office, but as soon as they arrived, Cade called Marcus. Judging by his side of the conversation, he wasn't getting the answers he'd hoped for.

Cade slammed the phone on the desk. Karli jumped at the noise and obvious anger.

"Are you okay?"

"No," Cade snapped.

Karli recoiled, understanding even though she didn't like the reaction.

"I'm sorry. Marcus wasn't much help. I shouldn't be taking it out on you."

"Or your desk."

Cade breathed a laugh. "True. Or Marcus. I know he's just doing his job. I hate all of this. A man is out there killing people and we're just waiting for him to stick his head out of the fucking hole he's hiding in."

"What did Marcus say?"

Cade sighed and dropped onto the chair next to Karli. "Not much. It's an open and active case, so he can't share anything that isn't public information."

"Understandable. He knows we were there earlier in the day and believe that area to be where Damon operates from."

Cade nodded. "He said they searched the warehouse we told him about. It was just a warehouse. No one was there who wasn't supposed to be. Being a Saturday, it was quiet. The offices were perfectly normal offices with managers who were all on the payroll. Nothing out of the ordinary popped up."

"Seriously?"

Cade shrugged. "I don't believe it either, but yeah."

"Who was in the vehicle we saw go in there?"

"The vehicle wasn't there when the police arrived. No one seemed to have any idea what they were asking about."

"A black SUV arrives, then vanishes, and a body is left there. That's not suspicious."

"I agree."

"Did Marcus know anything about the woman?"

"No. Nothing he could share, at least. He said she appeared to have been dumped there but killed elsewhere. They're not sure where yet. And she clearly suffered physical trauma. So far, he doesn't have an identity on her. That's what he said."

"You don't believe him?"

"I don't know. If they know who she is, they will contact the family before they'll release the name. He could have been telling the truth about not knowing her name yet, or he could know and not be able to tell me."

"Yeah, but if he knew and couldn't say, I think he would have told you that."

Cade shrugged. "Either way, we don't know anything about her. Or about what happened. Or about what the warehouse actually does."

"Didn't you look up the public records on the place?"

"Yeah, but it's a distribution center for a manufacturing parts company. They use it to hold items that customers need in a short period of time. It's an agreement they have with their top tier customers. The customer pays a premium to have certain parts delivered in a shorter time period. The place doesn't do a lot. They just house parts."

"That's smart."

Cade nodded. He stared across the room at the window behind his desk. Karli saw the lines around his eyes and the tension in his shoulders. He was relaxed and free when they left his apartment that morning, but now he was tense and frustrated.

"I'm going to go for a walk. I need to get out of here and clear my head." Cade surged to his feet and rested his hands on his hips.

"Okay."

He turned back to her. "Do you want to come with me?"

She shook her head. "I think you need a few minutes alone. If it's okay with you, I'll stay here and keep working. Maybe do some more research on that warehouse company."

Cade nodded absently. "Okay. Sounds good. I won't be long. I'll lock the doors. Don't go anywhere."

Karli smiled. "I won't."

Cade squeezed her hand, then left the office. A minute later, the door closed.

Karli drew a deep breath. She exhaled, surprised by how loud she was in the silent office. She stood there for a minute, listening to the sounds around her. Birds outside the window, vehicles every so often on the road outside. A horn. The whir of the computer.

It was strange to be alone. She hadn't been alone since she showed up on Stacey's doorstep. It felt like a lifetime ago. For years, Karli lived alone and the silence never bothered her. Living with Raina had been an adjustment. Learning how each other worked, what each other tolerated. They had their moments where one of them got quiet instead of angry because the relationship was important and making sure it survived mattered.

Karli never had those moments with Cade. They tiptoed around each other at first, but it didn't take long for them to settle into a comfortable and easy companionship. They could talk or be quiet. They could watch TV or read. They could kiss or hold hands. It was like they'd been together forever and knew what the other needed.

Cade walking out was good for him. Maybe it wasn't as easy for him to have her invade his space. She brought the hell to his doorstep. He might have invited her in when he followed her and approached her at the high school, but he didn't sign up for all of it. Not really.

Karli knew they needed to end this. Find Damon and Edie and move on. Figure out a way to live their lives, together or separate, without the ghosts of others haunting them.

Karli sat in her chair again and woke up the computer she'd been using. As soon as the screen appeared, she realized Cade had done all of the research on the company that owned the warehouse. She didn't even know the name of it.

She stood and went to his desk, looking for the notepad he was constantly writing on. It wasn't on his desk, but she knew it had to be there somewhere because he was always making notes in it. She hesitated for a second, then opened the first of his desk drawers to look for it.

The notepad wasn't in his desk. She spotted his computer bag on the floor underneath and looked inside, smiling when she saw the yellow pages. She carried the notepad back to her table and scanned the page Cade had been writing on for the company name. Right at the top with a line under it. Karli typed the company name into the search engine and waited for the results to load.

She sighed as she read one after another boring article about Bradbury Supply. They had manufacturing facilities in two US states and three countries. They shipped worldwide and produced a number of products that meant nothing to Karli.

She clicked through the About the Company tab and

read the meager information shared there. There were pictures of all the executives and short bios on each of them. None were of much interest or help.

Karli slapped the computer closed in frustration. Another dead end. There had to be a connection, but she had no idea what it could be. Or maybe there wasn't a connection, and it was all a coincidence that a woman was found in the exact same area where they were looking for Damon.

Karli stood and paced the room. It was small but moving helped. She was less annoyed by the endless string of useless information they were uncovering.

She walked past the table again and her hip bumped Cade's notepad. It slid off the table and flopped onto the floor, the sound loud enough to startle Karli in the otherwise silent office.

She picked up the notepad and flipped it over. Her name was written in red ink with a circle around it.

"What the hell?" Karli breathed.

She fell to her chair in a heap, scanning the page covered in Cade's neat, slanted handwriting.

Karli Sloane was circled. So was *Raina London*. There were lines drawn from both of them to *Damon Street* at the top of the page. And under their names was a list of things Cade apparently knew about each of them.

Address, phone number, job. But then there was more, like Karli's routine when she was hiding. Details of her appearance, including the birthmark on her neck. Where she grew up, who her parents and brothers were, and where she went to school since kindergarten.

He had all the same for Raina, except he didn't have anything about where she'd been staying since Tonya was killed. Karli breathed a sigh of relief that he hadn't figured that out.

She flipped the page over and scanned the next few. Cade had taken all kinds of notes on her. The next time she saw her name was a page where he wrote something about her similarities to Tonya. Then he questioned whether she was alive or Tonya. Then she saw the words that chilled her to her very core.

Karli killed Tonya?

"What are you doing?" Cade barked from right behind her.

Karli jumped and dropped the notepad. It hit the table and flopped onto the floor, facedown. She bent to grab it, but Cade was faster and reached it first.

"Were you going through my things?"

"I... I was looking for the name of the company that owns the warehouse. I wanted to do some research."

"And you decided to look through my stuff?"

Karli wasn't sure how to react to his abrasive behavior. "I thought we were working together. I didn't realize it would be an issue."

"For you to go through my things?"

"Well, I'm glad I did since you clearly don't trust me."

"What are you talking about?"

"You still think I killed Tonya?"

Cade's face paled beneath his beard. He turned the notepad over and saw the page Karli had been looking at before he walked in. "That was from weeks ago. When you were hiding. I thought you killed Tonya when she broke into your apartment."

"But you never bothered to cross it out? Do you still think I killed her?"

"No, of course not."

"So, why didn't you cross it out?"

Cade shrugged and set the notepad down. "I just didn't. I moved on. You walked in here and I realized there's no way you'd be coming to me if you were guilty. Especially since I knew you weren't the dead one."

Karli wasn't sure how to react to his admission. There was a part of her that understood why he would think she could have had something to do with Tonya's death, but after all the time they'd spent together, did he still think it could have happened that way?

"What about the front page? Where you have my name and Raina's tied to Damon?"

"You have a connection to him. It might not be what I assumed, but you have a connection."

"Yeah, he wants me dead."

"I know."

"So, why do you have all that personal information about me?"

He shrugged. "Once I figured out you were alive and Tonya was dead, I looked into you."

"You looked into me? You researched me?"

"Of course."

"You make it sound like that was expected."

"Are you honestly going to tell me you didn't look into me before you showed up in my office? That the day you walked in here, you didn't know anything more about me than what I told you that day at the football game or in the grocery store."

"Football game? Wait, grocery store?"

Cade softened just slightly. "The one you thought was a baseball game. They were actually playing football."

"You said baseball."

Cade shook his head. "No. I asked you about baseball

because I knew you weren't really there for the game. If you'd told me off and said it was football, I would have left you alone and assumed I was wrong about who you were. But you had no idea what was going on, so I knew you were only there to hide out."

"Dammit," Karli breathed. "Anyway, that doesn't matter. What matters is you were stalking me. You saw me at the grocery store?"

"I talked to you in the chips aisle two days before the football game."

Karli exhaled a mirthless laugh. She never put that together.

"I wasn't stalking you. I was trying to figure out if you killed my client."

"And we're back to that."

"I don't know why you're upset about this."

"Because it looks like you might still think it's true."

Cade shook his head. "No. I don't. But I also don't like you going through my things. I thought we trusted each other."

"You're the one who's acting like there's no trust right now."

Cade let out a sigh and shook his head. "Let's eat. I brought us lunch. I thought maybe that would clear our heads a bit."

Karli looked at the desk where he'd set the bag of food she hadn't noticed before. She nodded, feeling off-kilter and uneasy for the first time in days.

She couldn't have been wrong about Cade, but he wasn't acting like a man who wanted help. What else was he hiding in that notepad? And what else did he know about her?

14

WHAT ARE WE MISSING?

The question ran through Cade's head for the rest of the afternoon. The only time that wasn't what he wondered was when he asked if he'd been wrong about Karli the whole time. He didn't like either question. And didn't have an answer for either.

The warehouse was a dead end. The woman was an unknown. Damon, Raina, everything. He felt like there were answers, but he couldn't reach them. Like there was something right there that he wasn't seeing. He hated that feeling.

Cade and Karli barely spoke for the rest of the day. He was irritated with her. Not only did she go through his notes, but she went through his bag to find the notes. If she'd have asked, he would have told her the name of the company that owned the warehouse, but she didn't bother asking. She just helped herself to his personal stuff.

And then got mad at him for being frustrated that she invaded his privacy.

What the actual fuck?

He seethed as he thought about it again, walking in and

finding her staring at his notes like she had a right to look at them. And when he asked her, she acted like he was the bad guy.

Cade knew what a person looked like when they were hiding something. And Karli was hiding something. When she accused him of keeping secrets, there was a look, for only a second, that told him she hadn't been completely honest with her.

What he didn't know was what she was hiding.

He sat at his desk after their nearly silent lunch and flipped back to the beginning of his notes. His cheeks burned at the things he wrote about her before he knew her, but he had to follow where the evidence took him. And at the beginning, it led him straight to her.

After the first page, where he had details about Karli, he kept flipping. Following his original thought process and starting over was the only thing he could think to do. Even though he no longer thought Karli had anything to do with Tonya's murder, he was sure there was more to the story. There was something Karli wasn't telling him.

He kept going through his notes, finding very little about Silver, the man who did kill Tonya and who was then killed in the police station. Silver was an evil man, but didn't appear to be connected to Damon beyond killing Tonya and trying to get information about Raina. Living in the same building as Karli and Raina was the link, and his background appeared to have been a lucky coincidence. For Damon.

Cade kept going through his notes, at times stopping to trace his jumbled thoughts that led him to new conclusions. He was all over the place. He had theories on everything from corrupt cops to organized crime to Raina being the mastermind behind the whole thing. The problem was

Cade had no idea which theories were right and which were complete shit.

He worked himself in circles the rest of the day and jumped when his phone rang, yanking him out of the distracted state he was in.

"Yeah?" he answered, barely looking at the screen before answering.

"We got an ID," Marcus said.

"On the woman?"

"Yeah. Her name was Isabella Gallagher. She was reported missing two years ago."

"Fuck," Cade breathed. The poor woman.

"It gets worse. There were tracks up and down her arms, some scars worse than others, likely from being forced. She appeared to have been sexually assaulted before her death. And she had more drugs in her system than someone could survive."

"So someone loaded her up, raped her, and then dumped her once she was dead."

"That's our working theory."

"Jesus."

"Yeah." Marcus sighed heavily. "Listen, this is a big case. We're thinking about calling in the FBI. We don't have proof that it's human trafficking, but that's my assumption right now."

"Which means you'll be handing over the case and I'll never find Edie."

"Hopefully you will find her. But it'll be out of our hands if we end up turning it over."

"Shit. I need to find her. I can't let Tonya's death be for nothing."

"It wasn't for nothing. No matter what, it's helped us get

this far. She was in the wrong place at the wrong time, but she's opened up a lot we didn't know about."

"Like your corrupt cop," Cade spat.

"Yes, like that."

"Have you arrested someone yet?"

"We still don't know who it was. And if I knew, I wouldn't be able to tell you."

"Fine."

"If I learn anything else I can share with you, I'll let you know."

"Yeah. Thanks." Cade hung up, feeling like his skin was too tight. Nothing about the case was going the way he'd hoped.

"Was that Marcus?" Karli asked.

He'd forgotten she was there for a minute. Instead of meeting her gaze, he focused on his notepad and wrote down everything Marcus told him. "Yeah. They got an ID on the woman. She'd been missing for two years."

"Oh, my God."

"Yeah. She was put through hell. And I know she wasn't the only one. There are others out there. Others like her who have been abused and drugged and treated like property. They deserve better."

"I agree. We have to find Damon and get rid of him."

"I will."

Karli's quick breath in was audible and lifted Cade's head. She looked hurt before she neutralized her features into a careful mask. She nodded sharply, then went back to whatever she was doing on the computer.

An hour later, Cade finally had enough and asked if she was ready to leave. She nodded and gathered her things wordlessly. They went to the SUV and back to his place, neither of them speaking.

Cade's restless energy had him dying to get out of there and burn off the energy. He changed quickly into running clothes and told Karli he was going to go out, not giving her the option to ask where he was going or if she could go with him.

Cade's feet pounded the pavement, the rhythm echoing in his mind. Had it only been that morning when he thought they were getting closer? When he'd been sure things were moving in the right direction?

Waking up with Karli messed with his mind. He let great sex and a woman who made him confident get to him. He lost sight of reality and went with instincts again. The last time he'd done that, he found Alanna in bed with someone else.

He couldn't do it again. He couldn't stop who he was. His instincts were faulty. They had been since Alanna. Before Alanna. If he'd followed his gut with her, he would have known what was going on before he walked into her house and found her.

Karli made him think his instincts weren't wrong, but another woman was dead, and they were no closer to finding Damon Street. There was only one person alive who knew anything about him. One person who might be willing to help. Except she left town and wasn't talking.

Cade had to find her. He had to figure out where Raina went. Maybe she would talk to him over the phone. All he knew was she was the key to finding Damon Street.

DAMON PULLED up in front of headquarters and got out of the SUV. The circular driveway out front gave anyone inside the massive house a clear view of who was there before they got anywhere close to the house. The armed guards would be enough to scare off most people, but they barely gave Damon pause.

The one who did was the smirking son-of-a-bitch leaning against the doorframe like he owned the fucking place.

"I need to see the boss," Damon barked as he climbed the dozen steps to the front door.

Everything about the house was made to intimidate anyone who dared step foot on the property. A family home for generations, no one got through the gate at the foot of the driveway without a damn good reason. And even then, no one made it inside the house without an even better reason.

Damon hadn't needed a reason for either in more than a decade.

"The boss isn't available," Trevor said, not budging from his spot between Damon and the inside of the house.

"Too fucking bad. I need answers."

"And you're not going to get them."

Damon glared at the little fuck-face. Standing two steps below him put Damon at a disadvantage. He was never at a disadvantage. "Why the fuck not?"

"Because the boss has nothing to say to you."

"Excuse me?" Damon snapped.

"The boss is busy. Asked me to find out what you need."

"I need to know why a fucking body was dumped outside my office yesterday!" Damon's fury had him powering up the last two steps to get into Trevor's face.

Trevor didn't flinch. If anything, he looked as though he expected the outburst. "She was getting hard to control. Crying all the time and ruining the jobs she was supposed to do."

"Your little plaything is not my concern," Damon growled. He knew the woman was one of Trevor's the minute he saw her. She'd been with him more than once, cast to the side when Trevor was done with her, but always there for his demands. Trevor usually kept a few women for himself. Some he took out, others he kept locked up.

Damon enjoyed his moments with the women the Company brought in, but he'd never kept one of them as his own personal fuck toy. They were too strung out to be of much fun after they were used to test the latest drugs the Company intended to distribute. Trevor obviously didn't share Damon's opinion.

Trevor shrugged. "She's not my concern anymore either. I have a replacement."

"Why the fuck did you leave her body outside my office?"

"You were getting too much heat. You stopped being careful."

"What the fuck would you know?"

"I know you didn't kill the cop you were told to get rid of."

Damon snarled. "He's an asset."

"Are you sure about that? Because the boss disagrees. He's a loose cannon who can take down more than just you if he talks."

"He shares valuable information about cases the police department is investigating. He knows things."

"Like what?"

"Like Karli Sloane is still alive," Damon said with a smirk.

Trevor shrugged. "So?"

"So? So? She's a thorn in our fucking side. And she's a

witness. If she talks to the wrong person, she can bring down everything."

Trevor shook his head and pushed off the doorframe. He ran a hand through his greasy brown hair, pushing it off his cheek. "Karli Sloane doesn't know shit about the Company. All she knows about is you. Why should the Company care about that?"

"Because I know where all the bodies are buried. I've been in this business longer than anyone, including the boss. I don't think anyone would want me to talk."

Trevor moved down a step to get in Damon's face. He snarled before he spoke, his yellow teeth and foul breath putting Damon off before the words he spat sank in. "You say one fucking thing about anything and you'll wish you were dead. You know how this business works. You think you've got your cop in your pocket, but one word and you and your cop will disappear."

"Do you think I'm afraid of you?" Damon laughed at the thought. There was nothing Trevor could say or do that would scare him.

Trevor shook his head. "I don't really care if you're afraid of me or not. But I know what you want more than anything."

"Oh, yeah? And what's that?" Damon crossed his arms and looked up at the little shit. There was no way Trevor knew any damn thing. He couldn't piece together two thoughts without someone else telling him how to do it.

"You want to take over. You want to be in charge."

"So do you," Damon returned. They all wanted a chance to call the shots. It wasn't a big stretch to guess that.

Trevor leaned in. "Sure, but I'm not going to cross the boss to do it."

Damon swallowed roughly. Trevor's words landed a little too close. "You have no idea what you're talking about."

"No? You're probably right. I'm just the stupid little brother who was too dumb to really know what you and Clyde were doing, but I've been paying attention these last few years. I've been making the right moves. Starting with gaining the boss's trust. And promising to invest my own fortune in the company."

"What fortune?"

Trevor grinned. "Guess you haven't heard my old man is in a home now. It's only a matter of time before his fortune becomes mine. And the only thing the boss likes more than a good fuck is a boatload of cash."

"And you think that's going to solidify your place? If you bring in all your daddy's money?"

Trevor chuckled. "You have no idea who my father is, do you?"

Damon tried to think back. When he met Clyde, it didn't matter. They were both shitheads on the street and willing to do whatever it took to climb the ranks in the Company. When Clyde had to go, Damon didn't give a shit about his little brother.

"I'll give you a hint," Trevor said. "He owns half the city."

Damon gasped. Davis Developments was the biggest construction firm in the county. With a common name like that, Damon never considered it could be connected to Clyde and Trevor, but that knowledge was not welcome.

Trevor grinned like a cat surrounded by canaries. "When dear old dad dies, I'll get everything. The company, the holdings, all the investments, and a new place to move money through. The boss is smart enough to see how valuable my future contributions will be. What have you brought into the Company lately? Besides unnecessary attention and way too much recognition?"

Damon scowled. This was all Raina's fault. When she was with him, he was at the top of his game. He had everything. The boss was giving him more responsibility and trusting him. He had free rein and the trust of not only the boss but all the employees. He was the unofficial boss. Everyone went to him, not the boss. And he relished the power.

But now? Damon was without an office, without his guards, and he had a hell of a time getting a driver to bring him to see the boss. Who then refused to see him.

"I've been loyal to the Company for decades. There's no way I'm going to get kicked to the curb."

Trevor snorted. "No. You definitely won't be kicked to the curb. You might be dropped off on one, though. Maybe we can have your cop friend give you another dose of that stuff he gave you the other night. Then you won't even put up a fight when your employment ends."

Damon's blood boiled. How the fuck did Trevor know about that? "Are you spying on me?"

"Always." Trevor was unapologetic about it. He picked at his teeth and flicked away something. "It was worth it to watch you slump to the ground and piss yourself. I almost wanted to shake the man's hand. If I didn't want him dead. The boss and I watched it over and over again. It was too funny."

Damon snarled and got up in Trevor's face, grabbing his shirt. "How fucking dare you? You had no right to—"

"Don't you dare speak to me like that!" Trevor barked, brushing Damon's hands off him and sending Damon to his ass and rolling down the stairs. Trevor straightened his shirt and smoothed his hands over it.

Damon watched as the guards closed rank around Trevor, guns directed at Damon. His hip hurt like fucking hell where he fell. His shoulder was going to be bruised. Blood seeped into his hair from where he hit the back of his head on the steps.

"You are nothing. You have created more messed than you've cleaned up lately. And you will not make things worse for the Company. If you don't take care of the cop and forget about your whore of an ex, you will be the next one whose body the cops find. Find a new fucking office. And start doing your fucking job. Or I'll find someone else who will." Trevor turned and stormed back inside, closing the door with a finality that was as bad as one of the bullets Damon would be eating if he didn't get the fuck out of there.

Damon glared at the men pointing guns at him. Half of them were men he brought into the Company. Men who were loyal to him just a few months ago. But Raina ruined all of that. She made him look like a fool. She got away, and he was seen as a man who not only couldn't keep his woman in check, but couldn't even keep her in his possession. She was going to pay for what she did to his reputation.

And so was anyone else who got in his way. Starting with Karli Sloane.

15

———

KARLI STARED AT THE COMPUTER SCREEN AND TRIED TO MAKE herself invisible. It wasn't easy for a woman her size, but it was the only way she was going to get through the day without wanting to cry.

No. That wasn't true. She wanted to cry. But being invisible might mean she could get through the day without crying.

Things with Cade had been tense since he found her looking through his notepad. She really didn't know why it was such a big deal, but he'd barely spoken to her since. When he went out for a run the night before, she went to bed. She left the bedroom door slightly open, but he didn't join her. And when she woke up in the morning, he was already up and made coffee. While she took a shower, he got dressed, and they left without speaking. It had been the same all day.

So Karli put her head down and worked.

She was no help when it came to finding Damon, but Karli hoped maybe there was something about Tonya or Edie that could point her in the right direction. She scrolled through their social media accounts, finding when both stopped posting. Karli made notes of everything she thought could be helpful, including the last location posted for Edie. She frequented a local bar before she disappeared. It was doubtful anyone there knew anything, but Karli wrote everything down anyway.

After a silent lunch Cade ordered in, without asking Karli what she wanted, she went back to her research. She found public information about both women, including old articles from local papers about their successes in high school. Edie was a college tennis player who won a scholarship to a small local college. Tonya studied geology and worked for a company that watched seismic activity around the country until she took a leave of absence to look for Edie.

Karli copied posts Tonya shared on her social media pages about Edie's disappearance. Some of the comments were sympathetic, but others were cruel. Some downright threatening.

One person left comments on almost every post Tonya made. The comments ranged from *no one cares* to *I hope she'd dead*. Whenever someone tried to argue with the man, he attacked them and they disappeared from the comments.

Karli knew doing so much from her own social media accounts was a risk, but she didn't know how else to gather information. She clicked on the man's name and read his profile, being careful not to follow him or like anything he said.

He was a local, and if his photos were any indication, he was a regular at the same bar where Edie hung out before she disappeared.

It couldn't possibly be a coincidence.

Before Karli could think twice about what she was

doing, she picked up the phone and called Marcus from Tonya's borrowed phone. She saw Cade watching her out of the corner of her eye, but she didn't look at him.

"Patrick," Marcus said as he answered.

"Hey, Marcus. It's... me. I have been looking into Edie a bit and found something on some of Tonya's posts. I know you guys investigated and found no evidence that there was any foul play, but this guy is pretty vocal, and I think he was a regular at the same bar where Edie used to hang out."

"Hang on. Let me pull up the file." There were a few clicks on the other end before he spoke again. "Okay. Bernard worked on this one. He doesn't have notes about anything online. It's possible the posts were made after he did his initial investigation. He went to her apartment and her job and didn't find anything. Her car was never found, so it looked like she just left."

"Did he talk to anyone? Did he interview people who knew her?"

Marcus sighed. "You know there's only so much I can share."

"I know, but you can tell me if he talked to a man named Oscar Hyatt."

"Excuse me?" Marcus barked.

"Sorry. Do you need to go?" Karli asked.

"No. Did you say Oscar Hyatt?"

"Oh, yeah. I thought you were talking to someone else. You sounded mad. Do you know him?"

"He was... Yeah, I know him."

"Who is he?"

"He was the abusive ex-husband of someone who stayed at the shelter. After Holly left, he found her and killed her."

"Is he in jail?"

"He's dead."

"What?"

"He was found dead in an apparent suicide, but I don't think he killed himself."

"Why not?"

Marcus sighed again. His voice was softer when he spoke. "I think he was working for Damon. He got stupid and killed Holly, then Damon killed him. Holly was at the shelter at the same time as Raina."

"Wait, is this the Holly that Stacey talked about?" Karli gasped.

"Yeah, it is."

"Holy shit."

"Yeah. Which makes me think Damon really does have Edie. Oscar was too stupid to keep his mouth shut, which was what got him killed. He thought he was untouchable. He killed Holly and took a necklace she wore. It was one-of-a-kind, then Oscar gave it to his daughter. She showed it to Stacey, and it was as good as a confession that he killed her."

"Oh, my God."

"What's going on?" Cade asked.

Karli jumped. She'd forgotten he was there.

"Was that Cade?" Marcus asked.

"Yeah." Karli put the phone on speaker. "You're on speaker, Marcus."

"Anyway, if Oscar was taunting Tonya, he probably knew something about Edie. But obviously we can't ask him. I'll talk to Bernard and have him dig into this case again. He might be able to dig up some new information we didn't have before."

"Okay. Thanks, Marcus. We'll talk soon. Say hi for me."

"Will do. Thanks for the tip."

They both said goodbye and hung up. Karli wanted to

get back into her research, but Cade towered over her like she'd done something wrong.

She took her time looking up at him, not giving into his far too tempting scent that had the power to make her weak.

"Were you going to tell me any of that?"

"You were right here when I called Marcus. It's not like I wrote it all down on a notepad and hid it from you." It was a low blow, one she probably shouldn't have delivered, but it was necessary. She was still hurt.

Cade scowled at her and cursed under his breath. "What did you find that made you reach out to Marcus?"

Karli spun her computer to show him. "I was looking at Edie and Tonya's social media pages. Edie tagged this bar a few times before she disappeared. Tonya posted about Edie disappearing, and almost every time, this guy made a comment. When I looked at his profile, he was at the same bar more than once."

"Why didn't the police pick up on this?" Cade hissed.

"Marcus said their investigation was likely before all of this was posted. Tonya didn't turn to social media and the public until weeks after Edie went silent."

Cade nodded, his lips pressed into a tight line.

"Anyway," Karli continued, "Marcus said they think this Oscar Hyatt guy worked for Damon. He killed his ex-wife and then supposedly killed himself, but Marcus thinks Damon might have killed him and made it look like a suicide."

"What the hell have we walked into?" Cade breathed.

Karli shivered at the thought. She was excited to find something new, something that might help, but Cade was right. If they were in the middle of an even bigger situation than they knew, she might not survive it. Pretending she was dead was only going to keep her safe for so long.

"What is Marcus doing?"

"He's going to talk to the officer who investigated Edie's disappearance and have him take another look at everything."

"Is that a good idea?"

Karli shrugged. "Why not?"

"What if that cop covered something up and that's why the investigation never went anywhere?"

Karli shook her head. "I think that's a stretch. Marcus said Edie's car was gone. It looked like she just left."

Cade stared at the computer screen where Edie's smiling face was front and center. She looked happy. She had short, wavy hair with blonde highlights, an upturned nose, and a bright smile. Her brown skin glowed in the off-the-shoulder top she wore. She looked like she was having fun in the picture. Like nothing could touch her.

Karli's heart broke for her. For the woman she used to be. Even if they found her, the woman in the picture was gone. She would never be the same. Not if she was put through the same hell as the woman whose body was found just days ago.

Damon Street was an evil bastard. He stripped women down and broke them, then killed them if they didn't appease him. Raina was lucky. If Cade was right, Raina was the only one. No one else got away from Damon.

"Tonya was convinced Edie was somewhere. That she wouldn't just leave and not tell someone where she was going. She was smart and reliable. She enjoyed her job and worked hard. Edie wasn't a flake. She was alone and an easy target for someone like Damon who preyed on women who had no one else. But Edie had someone. And if this Oscar guy knew anything, it means someone else does, too. We're going to find her."

Karli nodded at his confidence. He was so sure that she believed him. She had to. Because finding Edie meant getting one step closer to ending Damon and his reign of terror.

CADE HAD BEEN SO busy looking for Damon, he didn't think to look for Edie. He knew they were connected, but Karli finding a new link between Edie and Damon meant they were on the right track. They just had to keep going.

Cade dug into Oscar Hyatt and found out everything he could about the guy, including his place of employment before his death. He allegedly killed himself at the desk where he worked, but if Marcus was right and Damon killed him, then Damon might have been the one who got him the job.

Deeper and deeper, Cade dug into Oscar, the company, and hopefully Damon. He felt like he was getting close to something. Like he was right there. But he didn't know what.

Then he found it. One name. One connection.

"Holy shit," Cade breathed, leaning back in his chair.

"What?"

"Oscar Hyatt was hired by DOS Metal Fabrication."

"Okay? What does that mean?"

"DOS is Damon Oliver Street."

"What? He was dumb enough to use his name?"

Cade nodded. "It's a corporation, but it's him. It has to be. The paperwork for the corporation is public record."

"He signed it?"

"No. But his mother did. Thirty years ago."

"What? Wait. I'm confused."

"It looks like Damon's mother owned the company. She named it for her only son. Damon even worked there for a while, but he's not listed on any of the official company records. Oscar Hyatt was found there by Stacey Allen. The cops ruled his death a suicide based on a note they found on the computer. But Oscar's prints were only on the desk and the computer. They didn't find any in any other part of the room or the building."

"But if he'd only been working there for a short time..."

Cade shook his head. "I don't think he was working there at all. He had another full-time job. One he was going to consistently. I think the DOS job was a cover for killing Oscar."

"Who are these people?" Karli whispered.

"As far as I can tell, they're ruthless and evil and will stop at nothing to get what they want and do what they want. Your friend Raina is lucky she's free of them."

Karli nodded absently. She chewed on her lower lip. Her eyes were glazed and unfocused as she stared off.

"What does all of this mean?" Karli asked a minute later.

"It means we have something new on Damon. We can look into the company. He probably uses it to move money and whatever else he wants. I'd guess they move drugs and women using company trucks. They might have other companies, but it only takes one break to crack open a case."

"And you think this could be it?" Karli asked. Her brown eyes gleamed with hope.

Cade nodded, a smile breaking free for the first time in days. "Yeah, I do. I really think this could be what we needed to put more pressure on Damon and to uncover some of the things he's involved in."

"And find Edie."

"Yeah. And find Edie."

Karli wrapped her arms around her middle, and Cade's frustration with her popped like a balloon. He strode to her, pulling her into his arms for the first time in far too long.

She sighed, the sound like all the tension in her body was released at once, and sank into him. She pressed her nose to his chest and inhaled deep. Her arms wrapped around his body, and she took a step closer, leaning on him and letting him give her his strength.

Cade held her tight, banding his arms around her and kicking himself for ever letting her go. They needed to talk. He needed to apologize. But first, they needed food. He could hear her stomach growling.

"Dinner?" he asked.

She nodded.

"Let's go. We'll pick something up on the way home. We can finish all of this tomorrow."

"Are you sure? You don't seem like you like to leave things undone."

"I don't, but tonight, I need you."

She smiled up at him, the light back in her beautiful face. He leaned down to kiss her, smiling when she met him halfway.

The kiss was electrifying. Like touching a live wire. He groaned, wanting her right then and there, but her stomach rumbled again and he stepped back reluctantly.

"I need to feed you. Then we'll finish that."

Karli nodded, nibbling on her lip. She kept her arm around him as he locked up and led her to the SUV. Not touching her or kissing her for twenty-four hours shouldn't have been so painful, but it had been. He loved seeing her smile again. He loved... a lot of things about her.

She ordered food while he drove, and they picked it up and were at his place in less than twenty minutes. They carried dinner inside and he unpacked it while she went to use the bathroom.

They sat on the couch, their legs touching while they ignored the TV and talked about everything they'd learned.

"How did Raina get away from Damon?" Cade asked. It was a question he'd wondered about for a long time. Damon didn't seem like the type of man who would let a woman leave him. But Raina did it.

"The night she left, he beat her badly. He'd hit her before, but the first time wasn't nearly as bad, and she only left for a day. She told me she got out of the apartment and went to a shelter, but he called her and convinced her it was because he'd been drinking and was angry about something with work and it would never happen again. She believed him and went back. Things were okay after that, but then he started locking her in the bedroom and limiting how much she could go out."

"Controlling her."

"Yeah. Taking away everything and everyone she had so she was alone. When she finally left, he'd beaten her badly enough that she had a fractured orbital and three broken ribs. She had a pregnancy scare the week before and realized if she ever got pregnant, he'd turn the same abuse to the child. She wasn't willing to live like that, and she knew she'd never bring a child into that life."

"I can't blame her for that." Cade slid his hand over Karli's knee and rubbed circles on her jeans covered leg.

"Neither can I. She needed to go to a hospital, but she knew Damon wouldn't let her. He told her she'd be fine and locked her in the bedroom again. She had her phone and watched videos about picking locks."

"Seriously?"

Karli nodded, a look of pride on her face. "That's what

she said. When it finally opened, she was shocked, but she knew it was her one and only chance. He had gone out, and he left her alone, but she didn't know how long he'd be gone. She got dressed in plain, dark clothes and got out of there. Their building had cameras, but she kept her head down and avoided them as much as possible. As soon as she was out of the building, she ran."

"Where did she go?"

"A women's shelter. She knew they would protect her. And they have. He knows she's there, but they've kept her safe."

"She's there?" Cade blurted. His fingers tightened on her knee. "She's there now? Still there?"

"Shit," Karli breathed.

"You've been lying to me."

"I couldn't tell you."

"Why not? Did you not trust me?"

"Like you didn't trust me to look at your notes?"

"That was different."

"How? How is it different that you take notes on the case we're working on together and won't share them, but I refuse to tell you where my friend is? The friend who you think is guilty."

"Because those notes are my train of thought. They're not intended to be shared. If you wanted to know something, I would have told you, but to go through my things—"

"I was just trying to help!"

Cade drew in a breath and let it out slowly, trying to calm his pounding heartbeat. "You knew I wanted to talk to her. You knew I thought she was the key to all of this. She knows where he lives. She knows things about him no one else knows. And you lied and told me she wasn't in town."

"Because if you knew, you wouldn't stop. And going in there would put her in more danger."

"You said he already knows where she is. How could she be in more danger?"

"Because she hasn't left in weeks. She's been locked inside since he sent the man who killed Tonya to kidnap her. The only times Raina's been out, she's been completely hidden. Damon will stop at nothing to get her back. Not because he loves her, but because she made a fool of him. And he's going to kill her for it."

Cade shook his head and stood. He stalked across the room, trying to make sense of it all. It didn't matter the reason, though. Karli lied to him. And that was the biggest red flag for him. He couldn't trust her. It didn't matter how he felt about her. It didn't matter that he liked having her in his space and in his life. That he was falling in love with her. He couldn't. Not if she was going to lie to him.

"I'm going to sleep at the office. I need to think things through."

"You're leaving?" she gasped.

Cade nodded. "You'll be safe here. You've been fine before. We haven't had any issues. I'll come back at nine tomorrow morning and pick you up. Keep the phone on so I can let you know when I'm on my way. Don't open the door for anyone else."

Karli crossed her arms and pursed her lips. She nodded sharply, staring at him.

He ached to change his mind. To go back to her and forgive everything. But he couldn't. Not now. Probably not ever.

Cade walked out of the apartment and down to his SUV. He tried to figure out a way to excuse what she did, but none came. By the time he made it to his office, he knew he'd made the right choice to leave. It hurt, and it would keep hurting, but trust wasn't optional for him. Not after what he'd been through with Alanna. If he couldn't trust Karli, they had to end whatever they were starting. Before he fell even deeper in love with her.

He let himself into the office and locked the door. He walked down the hallway toward his office, not noticing the light was on until he was almost to the door.

He wondered how they'd forgotten to turn off the light. He stepped into his office and stopped.

"What the hell are you doing in my office?"

"Waiting for you to arrive, Mr. Murray. Although I wish you'd have brought Karli Sloane with you. No worries. She'll come as soon as she hears I have you."

"Damon Street."

"I see my reputation proceeds me. Nice to meet you."

Cade snarled. "I wouldn't say the same."

Damon shrugged. "No bother to me. You won't be saying anything in a minute."

Cade turned just in time to see another man bringing the butt of a gun down on his head. Then everything went black.

16

Damon grinned as Cade Murray sank to the floor. Everything was going according to plan.

"What do you want to do with him?" Mick asked.

Damon rubbed his dry eyes and pushed aside the exhaustion he was feeling. He was not giving up now. Not when he was so close to having everything he wanted. Everything he deserved.

That bitch Karli was going to bring Raina right to him. And the idiot on the floor was the key.

"Put him in the trunk. We need to take him to the warehouse."

"The warehouse? I thought you didn't want to use it again. Not after the cops were all over it."

"Just do what I fucking said!" Damon was sick and tired of people questioning him. Didn't they know who he fucking was? He was going to be calling the shots soon. Everyone would see.

Mick grunted as he bent down and grabbed the unconscious PI.

Damon snorted. Not as smart as he thought he was. Cade Murray didn't see anything coming.

Mick carried Cade over his shoulder to the front of the building and out the door. Damon went through the office, collecting all the notes Karli and Cade made. He carried everything outside with him so no one else would find them. He couldn't risk the wrong cop seeing so much information about his operation.

He was not going down. Not now. Not ever.

Mick drove them to the warehouse and pulled inside the building. It was dark and vacant, just how it was supposed to be. Damon hadn't been back since fucking Trevor dumped the body outside, but he wasn't going to be chased out of his own office. Trevor could kiss his fucking ass.

Mick carried Cade inside and dumped him in a chair in Damon's office. Before the asshole could wake up, Mick zip-tied his wrists and ankles to the chair. Cade grunted, but he didn't open his eyes.

"What else do you need, boss?" Mick asked.

Damon shook his head and dismissed Mick. He was the only one who was still there. Who hadn't turned his back on Damon. The other fuckers had all turned tail and ran back to the boss. They were dead to him. But Mick was loyal.

Damon waited until Mick was gone to dig into Cade's pockets for his phone. He dialed the number he found in it for Tonya Warren. They were smart to have Karli use the dead woman's phone. But Damon was smarter. He figured out everything they'd done. From Karli sneaking out before Silver killed Tonya Warren to exactly who Tonya Warren was and why she was there in the first place. Their notes pieced together what he hadn't already uncovered, giving Damon the full picture.

No one was going to get the upper hand on Damon fucking Street.

"Cade?" Karli Sloane breathed into the phone. Alive.

"Sorry. Your boyfriend can't come to the phone right now."

"Who is this?"

"You should be dead, Ms. Sloane. If you were, everything would have worked out exactly how it was supposed to."

"Damon."

"I see my reputation proceeds me yet again."

"Your reputation is not something to be proud of."

"Oh, I disagree, Ms. Sloane. You think you know me, but you don't. You have no idea who I am or what I'm capable of." Damon growled, his anger steeping in. He hated the woman. He was going to take pleasure in killing her after he killed Raina and Cade Murray. But she was going to be the last one he killed. She was going to watch the others die because none of this would have happened if she'd just died like she was supposed to.

"What did you do to Cade?"

"Your boyfriend is okay. For now. He'll have a bit of a headache, but it's going to get so much worse for him if you don't do exactly what I tell you to do."

Karli sucked in a sob that made Damon grin. Good. She was already afraid. She would deliver.

He kicked Cade Murray's leg, smiling when there was a satisfying crack. Cade's eyes flew open as he screamed out in pain.

"Oh, look. He's awake," Damon said, injecting joy into his voice.

"Cade!" Karli shouted.

"Karli? What's going on?" Cade looked around like the woman was in the room with them.

Damon waved the phone at him. "I called her to say hi."

"Karli. Where are you? Did he hurt you?"

"No. I'm safe. Where are you?"

"Uh uh uh. None of that. You'll find out in just a minute. First, we need to talk, Ms. Sloane," Damon said, smiling at a scowling Cade Murray.

"What do you want me to do?"

"Bring Raina to me."

"No! I'll never."

"Then Cade will die. It's your choice, Ms. Sloane. Your boyfriend or your best friend."

"Don't do it, Karli. Don't listen to him."

Damon grinned at Cade. He expected the man's refusal. He knew they were fucking. When he found out about Cade helping her, he was sure the two of them were involved, and he was right.

"Aw, trying to protect her? Aren't you sweet?"

"Karli, you have to keep Raina away from him. He'll kill her. You know he will."

"But I'll kill you if she doesn't bring Raina to me," Damon said with a grin.

"That's not fair," Karli wailed.

Damon laughed, a dark, evil sound that bounced off the walls of the silent office and echoed back around him. It made him laugh harder to hear it. "I'm not sure who told you life was fair, Ms. Sloane, but they were wrong."

"Cade?" Karli whispered.

"Stay away, Karli. Don't come here. There's no way I'm getting out of here alive, no matter what he says. I'm sorry I left tonight. I should have listened to you. We should have talked."

"Oh, enough of this. Bring her to me!"

"I love you, Karli. Don't do it. I love you."

Damon punched Cade in the face, his nose breaking and blood pouring instantly down his face.

"Fuck!" Cade bellowed.

"What happened? What did you do?" Karli screamed.

"You have until dawn, Ms. Sloane. Bring Raina to my warehouse. You know, the one you drove by Saturday afternoon."

"I—"

"Don't have a choice, Ms. Sloane. His life for hers. See you soon."

Damon hung up the phone and smiled. She would show. He had no doubt. And when she did, he'd have so much fun.

KARLI'S HANDS shook as the phone disconnected. Tears streamed down her cheeks and her body felt like it was going to explode. Raina or Cade. There was no choice. She couldn't let either of them die. She loved them both.

Her heart pounded wildly. She unlocked the phone and scrolled through the numbers she'd called since she claimed the phone as her own. Only four people knew she had the phone. Only one of them could help.

Karli waited while the phone rang. It wasn't long before the person on the other end answered.

"Karli? Are you okay?"

Karli's voice broke on a sob before she could answer. "Frannie, Damon has Cade. And he's going to kill him if I don't bring him Raina."

"Oh, my God."

"I can't lose either of them. What am I going to do?"

"Where are you, Karli? Are you safe?"

Karli looked around the apartment and realized Damon likely knew exactly where she was. "I don't know. I'm at Cade's, but Damon found him. He has him. He was going to sleep at his office. He knew how to call me."

"Marcus is on the way. He'll be there soon. Stay inside with the doors locked. He'll tell you it's him. Do not open the door for anyone else. Do you understand me?"

Karli nodded. "Yes. I do. Thank you, Frannie."

"You're welcome. I'm going to stay on the phone with you until Marcus gets there. He shouldn't be long."

"Thank you, Frannie. I'm sorry."

"What in the hell are you sorry for?"

"For everything. If I'd have just left all of this alone—"

"That man is an evil bastard who kills for sport. I know. I saw it. He enjoys it. He delights in it. And he'll kill anyone who gets in his way. But we're not going to let him have Raina. She got away from him. She left. She's stronger now. But he's still a threat to her. It's not fair. And we're going to take him down."

"How?"

Someone knocked on the door before Frannie could answer. "Karli, it's Marcus."

"That's him. He sent me a text, too. In case we were still talking."

"Okay. Thank you, Frannie." Karli went to the door and opened it a crack.

Marcus was on the other side, looking tense but ready for anything. "Are you okay?"

Karli nodded. "Better. Thank you."

"Is that Frannie?"

"Yeah."

"I got her, babe. We'll be back soon."

"Good. I'll see you soon, Karli," Frannie said.

"Thank you. Bye." Karli hung up the phone and stepped back for Marcus to enter.

"Do you need to get anything? Any personal belongings?"

"Are you saying I won't be able to come back here?"

"I don't know, Karli. But if there's anything you need, I'd take it now."

Karli sucked in a breath and looked around the place she'd called home for the last week. Cade's apartment had become her respite. When she had nowhere else to go, he took her in. He put his own life on the line to help her get answers. To protect her.

And now he could die for it.

The emotions welled up inside Karli and spilled over. She nearly collapsed onto the floor before catching herself and stumbling to the couch. She put her head in her hands as the tears fell.

"We'll find Cade. I promise."

"I know where he is. Damon told me. But the only way he'll let Cade go is if I give him Raina."

"That's not happening," Marcus said, his voice steely.

"I agree. But I can't lose Cade either. I don't know what to do."

Marcus looked at her closely. Indecision warred in his face for a minute before he crossed the room to her and sat on the couch next to her. "You stop that fucker. You get up off this couch and you fight back. You come with me to talk to Frannie and you find a solution that means everyone walks out of there, except Damon. It's time for him to pay for his crimes."

"You want us to kill him?"

Marcus shook his head. "No. That's far too kind for a man like him. I want him to suffer in jail. To sit for a lifetime and think of all the people he killed. To remember the lives he took and give the families of his victims peace. They deserve that."

"Is that a punishment for him? He sounds like he enjoys killing people. Even Frannie said that."

"He does. I believe that. He really does. But knowing he can't do it ever again will drive him insane."

"Or he'll kill people in jail."

Marcus stared straight at Karli. His lips were a thin line, his gaze dark and dangerous. "There's a chance of that, but he won't get away with it. Prisons have their own systems for dealing with people who don't play by the rules."

Karli sucked in a breath. "I can't say I'd be disappointed if something happened to him."

"Neither would I. But first, we have to catch him."

Karli nodded. He was right. Cade believed they were going to find Damon. And Edie. It might not have happened the way they hoped, but Karli knew exactly where Damon was, and where he would be until dawn. Now all they had to do was bring him in.

Marcus walked out of the apartment first, shielding Karli until they got to his police car. They rode in mostly silence until they got to Shelter in the Storm. Marcus parked in the back, then got out and came around to open Karli's door. He led her inside.

Karli heard multiple voices before she turned the corner into a kitchen. She'd only been to the shelter once, before Raina left, when Stacey wanted to talk to her about Raina moving in. The kitchen wasn't familiar to her.

But the four women around the table were.

"Frannie," Karli breathed. "You called them?"

"Of course," Frannie said. "Why would I not?"

"I'm going to give myself up," Raina said.

"That's why," Karli said, glaring at Frannie. "You can't do that, Raina."

"Why not? He wants me. He's doing all of this because of me. Why would I let the man you love die?" Raina jumped up from the table and hurried over to Karli. She wrapped her arms around her, standing on her tiptoes to do it. "I won't let Cade die for me."

Karli sucked in a breath. Raina's words hit her square in the chest. *The man she loved?* Karli couldn't deny that. *And letting him die?* That hurt too much to even consider.

"I won't let you die for him. Neither will he. He told me not to let you come."

"You talked to him?" Stacey blurted.

Karli nodded as Raina took a step away from her and grabbed her hand. "He was there when Damon called me."

Everyone asked questions at once, talking over each other.

Frannie whistled, capturing the attention of everyone. "Sit. All of you. Karli, start at the beginning and tell us everything."

Karli nodded and took a seat. They all filed around her, listening to her detailed recount of the call from Damon. When she'd finished telling them about that, they asked why Cade was at the office instead of home with her.

"We got into a fight."

"About what?" Raina asked.

"He found out you were here. That you hadn't left town like I said you did."

"And he got mad?" Jessica asked.

"His ex cheated on him. He only found out when the wife of the guy she was sleeping with hired Cade to get proof the husband was having an affair. They were going through a divorce and he was trying to screw her out of everything, so she hired Cade. When he found the evidence, the husband claimed he'd been set up by Cade and the girl-friend and had all the evidence thrown out. The woman got nothing, the husband got away with it, and Cade got blackballed."

"Fuck," Stacey breathed.

"I heard about that," Frannie said. "That was... bad. I didn't realize it was Cade. I believed the cheating son-of-a-bitch. I really thought he was set up. He had a damn good lawyer to convince people it was all a trap."

"Apparently, but for Cade, it means he has a hard time trusting anyone. He almost lost his entire business. That's why he took Tonya's case. It was a last ditch effort to make some money."

"And now he's being held by the man who's created hell for everyone in this room," Raina said.

They all nodded.

"No more," Raina declared. "I can't let him do it. I'll give myself up and he'll stop all of this."

"No," the others said in unison.

"I can't let him continue. I just can't. He's killing people to try to get to me. He's ruining the lives of my friends. He won't stop until I go back to him. If I do it, he'll stop."

"You know that's not true," Frannie said firmly. "Damon is the most evil man I've ever met in my life. The first time I saw him, I knew. But when I was face-to-face with him and believed he was going to kill me... I've never known evil like him. He doesn't care who he hurts or what he has to do to get what he wants."

"So, what does he want?" Jessica asked.

"Me," Raina declared. "That's all he wants."

"No," Stacey said. "You're a means to an end. He doesn't want you. He wants what you took from him."

"I didn't take anything from him," Raina declared.

"That's not what she means, honey," Frannie said. "She means you walking away made him look bad. It made others question his authority or his manhood or something. He doesn't care about you. I'm sorry, but he never did. You know that. A man who cares about you will never raise a hand to you. He will never hurt others to get to you."

"I know," Raina whispered.

"We know we can't let him have Raina. So, what can we do?" Stacey asked.

"We expose him. We take away everything he has left. We force him out of the shadows and put his face everywhere. Cade said no one really knows what he looks like. He was desperate to talk to Raina because she's the only person who's ever walked away from Damon and lived. So, we tell the world who he is." Karli met the gazes of the others around the table and knew it was the best plan.

But they only had a few hours to figure out exactly how to do it. A few hours to expose him, save Cade, and protect Raina.

17

———

Karli was going to be sick. Swear to God. Her stomach rolled at the thought of what she was walking in to. Why did she think this was a good idea?

The entire block was dark. Faded street lights tried to break through the inky blackness, but they failed as miserably as Karli feared she would fail.

Everything in her told her to turn around and run. Get the hell away from there. Away from certain death. She wanted to. She could disappear. Vanish into the night like she did when Tonya broke into her apartment. Walk away. Hide. Never show her face again.

She sucked in a breath and told that scared woman inside her to shut the fuck up. She wouldn't be able to live with herself if she ran again. The first time, she wasn't leaving someone behind, not knowingly. She didn't walk away from someone she loved about to be killed. She couldn't do that. She couldn't let Cade die.

Karli inched closer to the building where Damon told her to go. She was hours early, but she wanted to catch him by surprise. The entire plan hinged on Damon not knowing she was there. Or that she wasn't alone.

The building only had three ways inside. None of them had ever been in there, so they were planning their attack without knowing what they'd be walking in to.

The building was searched when the body was found, but Marcus hadn't been with the team. All he knew was there was a large open work area with offices toward the back of the building. The assumption was Cade was being held in one of those offices. Likely not the one with a door to the outside, but if he was in that room, Frannie was going to be the first one to see Damon. And Cade.

Karli adjusted the mask they'd given her. The edges were scratchy against her skin, but the inside was soft. Flecks of sparkles came off on her fingertips when she touched the black mask. The others told her it was for luck. And for strength. Wearing it was supposed to make her feel like she could do anything. Take away her fear. Give her nothing but courage.

The mask must have used up all its good energy because Karli was so scared she thought she was going to pee herself.

Karli reached her entry point and waited. She was the first one to go inside. She was the only one Damon expected. The others tried to argue with her, but Karli insisted. Damon tried to have her killed. She wanted to look him in the eye and tell him he failed. And he would keep failing because she wasn't going down so easily. She was going to fight. She had people to fight for. She would not lose.

With a deep breath, Karli opened the door. She nearly cried with relief when it opened silently and she was able to get inside the building without announcing her presence.

There were lights on toward the back of the building

where the offices were. The main work area was dark, with high overhead lights dimmed low for the nighttime.

Karli kept to the wall, walking slowly. She had to confirm Cade and Damon were there, then text Marcus. Marcus had a team on standby. And right behind them would be the media, ready to cover the story of a deadly kingpin getting locked up.

Voices captured Karli's attention in the second office. One louder than the other. She was too far away to make out what they were saying, but it didn't matter. She found Cade.

Cade was in a chair in the first office. He was alone. The door was open, and no one else was inside. Karli's pulse raced with excitement. She couldn't believe it. He was there. And all she had to do was get him out and they would be free.

"Cade," she whispered, dropping to her knees in front of him.

He jerked back, her voice waking him. "What— Karli. Why are you here? I told you not to come."

"I had to. There was no way I was going to leave you here. He's going to kill you." Karli tugged at the zip-ties on his ankles. They were tight, and not budging. "We have a plan. But I need to get you out of here."

"It's too dangerous. He's going to kill all of us. He was never going to let me go. Where's Raina? Please tell me you didn't bring her."

Karli shook her head. "No. She's safe."

"Good. I'm sorry I got upset with you for not telling me she was in town. I shouldn't have. You were right to keep it from me. I would have put her in more danger than I already did."

"You didn't do this. Shit. Why won't these come off?" Karli hissed. She pulled the knife Marcus gave her out of her waistband and opened it. The soft click of the blade locking in place seemed loud in the quiet office.

Karli looked up and found Cade asleep again. He already had bruises around his eyes. Dried blood caked his face and onto his shirt. The kink in his nose wasn't there the last time she saw him.

Damon.

Tears fought Karli, but she didn't have time to get upset about what Damon did to Cade. She had to get him the hell out of there. Get him to safety. The others would understand.

Karli slid the blade between the zip-tie and the leg of the chair. It was thick and took her a minute to cut through the thing and free Cade's leg. She glanced back at the door, listening for the voices in the next office, then went to work on his second leg.

With both legs free, Karli breathed a sigh of relief. She was making progress. Even if Cade was unconscious at the moment, she could wake him up and get him out of there.

Adrenaline pulsed through her, keeping Karli focused on her task. She managed to get the first zip-tie off his wrist, but she heard a noise outside the office when she started to work on the second one.

A door closed. Somewhere in the building. Maybe one of the exterior doors. Someone left.

Or someone arrived. And wasn't quiet.

Karli pulled out her phone and saw she had texts from Marcus, asking for a status update.

I'm with Cade. He's hurt, barely conscious. Tied to a chair. Almost free.

Who left the building?

I don't know.

Have you seen Damon?

No. But there were two people talking. One of the voices sounded like him.

Okay.

Karli moved to the other side of the chair and started to cut through the last zip-tie. She alternated between watching the door and watching the strip of plastic, praying she made it through before anyone walked through the office door.

Victory! Karli nearly shouted with joy when the last zip-tie gave way and Cade was free. He grunted, his hand falling off the armrest and smacking her in the boob.

"Cade," she whispered. "We need to go. Cade. Wake up!"

Karli nudged him, sighing when he blinked his eyes open and smiled up at her.

"Hey," he said. His voice was far too loud and carried in the otherwise silent building.

"Shh," Karli hissed. "We need to get out of here before Damon comes back."

The other man's name woke Cade up and sent a glimmer of clarity to his otherwise unfocused eyes. Cade put his hands on the armrests and pushed himself to a stand, immediately losing his balance and falling onto Karli.

She caught him the best she could, her entire body taking his weight before he steadied himself and stood again.

"Fucking hell, my head hurts."

"I'm sorry. I never should have gotten you involved in all of this."

He shook his head, then winced. "Don't you dare say

that. I was already involved, and I would have been involved with or without you. Having you to work with gave me a gift I never thought I'd have. You showed me how to love someone. And I'll forever be grateful to you for that. Even if I only get to enjoy it for a few more minutes."

A slow clap started behind them. Karli jumped, spinning and screaming at the same time. Cade lost his balance and fell, landing in a pile on the floor at her feet.

"Isn't this so cute? You came to rescue him. And you thought you could just what? Walk out?" Damon laughed.

"That's exactly what I'm going to do," Karli said. She reached down for Cade to help him up again. Her hands trembled. She kept her gaze on Damon as Cade rose to his feet and leaned on her for support.

Damon just watched them, his arms crossed and a sickly smirk on his lips. When Karli and Cade took a step forward, his smile melted away and his arms fell to his sides.

"You're not fucking leaving. I told you to bring Raina. Where is she?"

"Did you really think she would come? That she would ever want to see you again?"

"I don't care what she wants!" Damon shouted. His voice echoed off the steel walls of the building. "Raina is mine. She's been mine since the first night she let me take her on a date. There's no escaping. She can either return to my bed or die. Those are the only two options she has."

"She found a third one and got away from you. She's never coming back to you."

Damon growled and lunged toward Karli. Cade tried to step in front of her. He swung at Damon and missed, rolling to the floor with a grunt.

"Cade!" Karli leaned down to see if he was okay, but Damon grabbed her hair. "Gah!"

"Where's Raina?" Damon snarled. Spit flew from his lips, landing on her cheek. He looked crazy and unhinged, two words she knew fit him even before Karli met the man.

"Raina's not coming. She's safe. Where you're never going to find her." Karli struggled to get free, but he had his fingers wrapped around her hair. He tugged harder at her curls, sending blinding pain through her head. Karli refused to cry out again.

"So, she's still at Shelter in the Storm? With that bitch, Frannie. I should have killed her years ago. Just put my knife to her throat and pulled. Did she tell you about the woman I killed in the alley? If I'd have known she was watching, I would have enjoyed it more. But now..." Damon yanked Karli to him and spun her around to face Cade. "Now, I have a witness when I kill you."

"Leave her alone," Cade barked, his voice weak and strained.

"What are you going to do about it?" Damon taunted him.

Karli fought against him until she felt the cold metal on her skin. If she swallowed, it would cut her. She was going to die. She knew it.

"I haven't been able to get my hands dirty lately. I've missed the feel of a blade between my fingers. A gun in my hand. The pulse of another person fading before death claims them. Of course, my favorite thing of all is the crunch of bones breaking." Damon kicked Cade, a sickening crunch splitting the air.

Cade clutched his ribs where Damon kicked him and rolled. He moaned in pain.

A sob threatened Karli. They were both going to die. It didn't matter that help was coming. Damon wouldn't let them live long enough for help to arrive.

"I'd planned to kill him first, Ms. Sloane. To let you watch him die. I thought it would be a good lesson for you that you should have just fucking died when you were supposed to. If you had, this would all be over by now because Raina would have come back to me. She would have known she had no choice."

"She always has a choice," Karli breathed, careful not to move her throat more than necessary.

"Not this time. No woman has ever left me, and no one else ever will. Raina was going to be the next one to die. Of course, I was going to be more creative with her. I wasn't sure if I was going to fuck her before or after I killed her. But I'll have her again. No matter what. Then it would be you. Slow. So you could suffer."

"You're sick."

Damon shrugged, the movement against Karli's back letting her feel where he was. "I think I'm like anyone else. You like art. Well, death is my version of art. It's beautiful. To see someone fight for something. To watch them fight to live. And to have the control to take it away from them. Why is that wrong?"

"Who are you to play God?"

"Who said I'm playing?"

"Drop the knife, Damon," Frannie said, her voice steady and steely.

"Ah, Francesca. We meet again. I was wondering when you were going to announce your presence."

Frannie stepped into the office, with Jessica and Stacey right behind her. All three of them were in solid black with masks on. Frannie held a gun. Stacey and Jessica had knives and pepper spray.

"We made it a party." Damon turned to Stacey, dragging Karli with him and keeping her body between them. "Mrs.

Allen, we haven't met, but you knew my associate Oscar Hyatt. Such a shame he took his life right before you had a chance to speak to him." He shifted to look at Jessica. "And Ms. German. Such a smart woman. I hope the police don't think twice about setting you free since their other suspect died under mysterious circumstances. It's funny how that keeps happening with all of you around."

"It's over, Damon," Frannie said. "There's no way out for you."

Damon snorted. "Is that really what you think? That I'm done. That you got me? I knew you were here the moment you arrived," he shouted.

Karli gasped. She thought they were being quiet. That they'd surprised him.

"Did you really think I'd tell you to come here and not have a backup plan for my backup plan? I have cameras everywhere. Let's see, Ms. Sloane, you came in the front door. Ms. German and Mrs. Allen came through the side door three minutes later. And Francesca, you came through the back four minutes after that. I had to wait for you to arrive before I could let Ms. Sloane know I was watching her. She had time to cut all the zip-ties on poor Mr. Murray. But no worries. He's not going to be a lot of help when I kill all of you." Damon looked at the three women by the door, using Karli as a shield. "We're still missing Raina, though. Are you really all ready to die for her?"

"You're the only one who's going to die tonight," Jessica snarled.

"Oh, my goodness. Ms. German. Don't let anyone hear you say that. If I end up dead, you'll be the prime suspect."

"Been there, done that," Jessica snapped.

Damon chuckled. "Such bravado in the face of death. Were you that strong when you went into Silver's apartment? I have to admit, I didn't think you would be smart enough to find him."

"Enough chitchat, Damon. It's time for you to go." Frannie stepped forward, her gun pointing just over Karli's shoulder.

Karli wanted the whole thing to be over. If they were all inside, why weren't the cops there yet? What was going on?

Karli felt a buzz against her back. Damon grunted, then bumped against her ass as he reached into his pocket. Karli tried to move away from him, but the knife kept her close.

The knife slipped for half a second before tightening against her skin. Damon shoved his phone back into his pocket and moved toward the wall with Karli having no choice but to go with him.

"You're right, Francesca. It is time for me to go. But I'm not going out the front where all your cop friends are waiting."

Frannie, Jessica, and Stacey moved toward them, stepping over Cade's silent and still body.

"Where are you going, Damon?" Frannie asked. Her gaze ran behind Karli, searching for Damon's escape plan.

He was going to get away. Karli knew it. He was close to an escape they weren't aware of, and he would disappear again. Raina wouldn't be safe until Damon was in jail or in the ground. Karli didn't care which.

She leaned forward just enough to get leverage, then slammed her head back against his face. He dropped the knife immediately and stumbled away from her.

"You bitch," he hissed, spitting blood at her.

Karli grabbed the knife on the floor, pointing it at Damon.

He held his nose, blood pouring down his face and

coating the vinyl flooring under him. "Do you think that's going to stop me?"

Karli backed up. The police would be there any second.

Almost on cue, doors slammed and lights flooded the place. Karli let out a sigh of relief. It was over. She turned to see the police streaming through the building toward them. She almost smiled.

The first cop through the door pointed his gun at each of them. "Where is he?"

Karli turned around.

Damon was gone.

18

DAMON KEPT TO THE SHADOWS AS HE MADE HIS WAY AWAY from the building. Those bitches thought they were so smart. Fucking women. Damon knew exactly what they were doing. He expected it. And he wasn't going to fall for it.

Mick was waiting for him three blocks away, outside the radius the cops set up. Bernard earned his keep once again telling Damon where the cops would be when he tipped him off that there was a plan to move on his office.

Damon was barely in the vehicle when Mick took off. Damon seethed the entire drive. All of his plans were ruined, and it was all Trevor's fucking fault.

Mick pulled up in front of headquarters. The gate opened for them like it always did. The place was dark, but Damon knew that didn't mean it was quiet. Headquarters was always running.

Trevor was at the front door when Mick stopped the SUV. His arms were crossed, his feet set wide. He looked angry at being interrupted. Fuck him. Damon was out of patience with the little fucker.

"What are you doing here?"

"This is all your fault," Damon snarled as he stalked toward the younger man.

A flash of unease went through Trevor's eyes before they went passive again. "What's my fault? That you can't follow fucking orders?"

"The PI, the dead woman, everything happening right now, is because of you and your fuck-toy!"

Trevor glanced back at headquarters, then took a step toward Damon. His face and voice hardened. "What are you talking about?"

"That whore you've been keeping around? Edie? The one you picked up months ago and decided to keep for yourself? She's the reason for all of this. The PI asked me about her. The woman who was actually killed was her cousin. None of this would be happening if it weren't for you sticking your dick where it doesn't belong."

Trevor advanced on Damon so fast, Damon didn't have time to dodge the younger man's attack. He grabbed Damon by the front of his shirt and slammed him against the stone wall lining the steps.

Damon grinned when he heard the cock of Mick's gun.

"Let go of him," Mick growled.

Damon smirked at Trevor. He had no choice. He would be dead if he didn't listen.

Trevor released Damon with a shove. He took half a step back.

Damon smoothed his hands down his shirt, pressing out the wrinkles the little fucker created. He looked up to thank Mick. Mick nodded, tucking his gun away just as a shot rang out in the silence of the night.

Trevor had a gun pointing at Mick.

Mick looked down, blood seeping through his shirt. He fell to his knees, one hitting one step and the other hitting lower. He rolled, his strength already failing. Trevor walked over to him and kicked him, shoving Mick the rest of the way down the stairs.

All Damon could do was watch as his last ally bled out on the driveway.

"Can't have him getting blood on the steps. The boss will be pissed. Now, what were you saying about all this being my fault? Because I'm pretty sure you were the one who ordered the woman to be killed. And you were the one who had the wrong fucking one killed. And you were the one who killed the waste of flesh who killed her. And then you were the one who refused to kill the cop who knew about all of it. What does this have to do with Edie?"

Damon started at Mick, his lifeless body facedown on the driveway. He was the closest thing Damon had to a friend since he killed Clyde. Mick was the only one who stuck by Damon. And the little fucker killed him.

"Edie's cousin hired the PI to find her. She was in the apartment and was mistaken for Karli Sloane. Karli Sloane and the PI are now even more determined to find Edie since her cousin was killed. They know she's here. They know she's one of yours."

"The only way they'd know that is if you told them. Did you tell them, Damon?"

"I didn't tell them anything. They know. They know all kinds of things."

"It sounds to me like someone's been talking. Someone who was supposed to do a job but didn't. Or maybe the cop is talking. Either way, I think it's time we tie up some loose ends, Damon. Sort of like you did when you killed my brother."

Damon slammed into Trevor as he fired, knocking his arm away before the shot could go off. Trevor fell onto the stairs, his head hitting the edge of one step. Damon would have enjoyed the sound if he wasn't about to be killed. He took off, knowing it was his only chance to get away from Trevor before he shook off the blow and tried again.

Damon got into the running SUV and tore away from headquarters. Shots rang out behind him, but none hit the vehicle. He kept going, whooping when the gate opened in front of him and he was off the property and free.

He drove, not knowing where to go. Mick was dead. Trevor was going to tell the boss Damon was a liability. He couldn't go home or to any of his usual places. They would find him. And Damon was not going down like that. He was not going to let Trevor be the one who took him out.

Damon still had a mission. Find Raina. And kill the bitch for fucking up his life.

From the moment the police swarmed into the room, Karli knew her time was ticking. Marcus assured her it would be fine, but cops weren't people you could trick easily. Especially not when her face had been all over the news for weeks.

The pictures of Karli the news shared were all actual pictures of her, not of Tonya, which meant everyone believed she was the dead woman. She heard the whispers as they processed the scene and searched for Damon's escape route. She heard the same whispers as she was escorted through the hospital, even with her head down, to Cade's room.

His room was quiet, though. Except the beeping of the machines monitoring him. Telling her he was still alive.

Karli hid in his room all night. Cade woke up a few

times, but when he did, it was only for a few seconds. The nurses assured her that was a good thing. They wanted his body to rest, but they wanted him to fight for consciousness.

Karli finally fell asleep sometime well after midnight. She crossed her arms and rested them on the side of his bed and sleep took her. Maybe it was being close to him, maybe it was the cop at the door, or maybe it was just exhaustion, but Karli crashed.

A croak and brush of a hand woke her up with a jolt. She sat up suddenly, looking around for who or what made noise. Her gaze landed on Cade and found him looking at her.

"You're awake," she breathed.

"Water," he whispered.

Karli grabbed the plastic pitcher a nurse filled with ice and water sometime during the day. It was no longer cold, but it was all they had. She poured a cup and held the straw steady as she brought it to Cade's lips.

He pursed his lips and sucked, then winced and reached for his nose. He winced again when he touched the bandages that covered his face.

"Damon?"

"He got away."

"Dammit." Cade made a move to get out of bed, but Karli pushed him back.

"Where are you going?"

"Find him."

"You can barely move. You're not going anywhere. The police will handle it."

Cade collapsed against the bed again and was asleep in seconds.

Karli didn't want to leave the room, even as she was

desperate to know what was going on. No one had been in to update her since she and Cade had arrived.

Karli couldn't fall back to sleep as easily as Cade had. She paced the room and watched the monitors and waited for the sun to come up. She left Tonya's phone at the shelter and Cade's phone was destroyed, so Karli was alone with her thoughts. And they were not good thoughts.

Someone knocked on the door shortly after the sun made an appearance in the morning sky. The soft knock told Karli it likely wasn't a nurse, and when the door opened and Jessica's face appeared, Karli nearly cried with relief.

"We brought breakfast," she whispered. "Is he still out?"

Karli nodded and waved Jessica and Braden into the room. "He woke up a few hours ago and wanted water. When I told him Damon got away, he tried to get out of bed, but just that little bit of movement knocked him out again."

"That's to be expected," Braden said softly. "How are you feeling?"

Karli shrugged. She'd been checked out the day before, like all of them, but she didn't have any injuries. "I'm fine. He didn't hurt me."

"That's not what I'm asking," Braden said. His hazel eyes bore into Karli's, like he could see deeper than skin level.

"I'm worried about Cade. And terrified about Damon."

Braden nodded. "I don't blame you. For either. Are you hungry? Food always helps."

"That's what Taylor says," Jessica said, looking up at Braden with so much love it ached inside Karli.

"Where do you think I got it from?" Braden's sister was Jessica's boss. Taylor was instrumental in the two of them getting together, and Karli felt immense gratitude toward her for bringing such happiness into Jessica's life.

Jessica reached into the bag they brought and handed a

sandwich to Karli. She was starving all of a sudden, forgetting when she last ate. Braden handed her a coffee, and she nearly cried with joy.

The three of them ate in silence, the sound of their chewing the only noise above the beeping machines.

"Is there an update?" Karli finally asked. She knew the answer before she asked it. Jessica would have led with news if there was any, but her silence told Karli no one had found Damon yet.

"The police know how he got out of the building. They think someone was waiting for him with a vehicle, but they're still going through cameras and trying to find something definitive." Jessica looked as happy as Karli felt with that news.

"Dammit. I really thought we had him. How's Raina?" Karli knew as bad as the whole thing was for her, it was worse for Raina. She was the one Damon was fixated on.

"She's scared. She doesn't know what she should do." Jessica met Karli's gaze, telling her how to read between the lines.

"She can not go back to him," Karli said firmly.

Jessica nodded. "We told her that. She doesn't want anyone else to die."

"What does she think will happen to her?"

"I know," Jessica said with a sigh.

They finished their food in silence. Braden collected their garbage and set the bag on the tray for disposal. They were finishing their coffees when a louder knock on the door had all of them turning toward it.

Braden jumped up and stood between the door and the rest of them. When the door opened, he demanded to see the badge of the woman trying to get in the room. She didn't argue with him and identified herself as

Rachel, the day shift nurse who would be taking over Cade's care.

She flashed a smile to Karli and Jessica, then focused on Cade. He was still sleeping. "Has he woken yet?" Rachel looked between Karli and Jessica, unsure which of them was there for Cade.

Jessica looked at Karli and let her answer.

"He woke up a few hours ago and asked for water. He tried to get up, but I didn't let him, and he fell asleep again."

Rachel nodded. "Good. He needs his rest. It looks like his vitals are good. Is it okay if I do a quick exam?"

Karli nodded and moved to the other side of the curtain with Braden and Jessica. Rachel spoke softly to Cade, encouraging him to wake up while she did her exam. Her voice got a little louder at the end, then she said, "Welcome back, Mr. Murray."

Cade groaned, and Karli's heart nearly burst.

"He's awake?" Karli gasped.

"He's awake. You can all come back," Rachel said.

Braden pushed the curtain aside for Karli to go to Cade. Rachel was helping him sit up with an extra pillow. She raised the top of the bed.

Cade looked like shit, but he was awake and alive. His eyes were sunken in and his face was bruised around his bandages. His skin was ashen where it wasn't bruised. He'd been through hell.

"The doctor will be in around nine for rounds. He'll do a more thorough exam. The broken ribs are the biggest concern, but it's manageable. You were lucky, Mr. Murray." Rachel smiled at all of them before she left the room.

"Damon?" Cade asked first thing.

"No news. He's still in the wind," Braden said.

"No one knows anything?" Cade croaked.

"You need your rest," Karli said.

"I will get plenty of rest. Someone needs to find him. He knows where Edie is."

"What?" Karli gasped.

"When he had me, I asked him about Edie. I figured he'd blow off my questions, but he answered me. He said he knew who I was talking about. Someone in the organization has her as his own toy." Cade's voice was scratchy and crackly, but the determination was clear.

"She's alive?" Karli asked.

Cade nodded. "That's what it sounded like. Edie is alive. And I'd be willing to bet Damon knows where she is. We have to find him."

"The police will," Braden said. "I'll update Marcus." He looked at Jessica. "We should go. Let Cade rest."

Jessica nodded. She hugged Karli tight. "I'm so happy you're safe."

"Me, too," Karli replied.

Jessica squeezed Cade's hand and smiled at them. Braden nodded to both of them. They walked out with their arms around each other.

"How the hell did he get away?" Cade asked.

"He knew we were coming. He must have had an escape plan."

"Why didn't the cops surround the building?"

"I don't know."

"Dammit. I don't know what I'm more angry about... the cops letting Damon get away or you risking your life for me."

"What? I saved you."

"You almost got yourself killed. I'd never be able to live with myself if anything happened to you."

"That's how I felt, too."

Cade reached for her hand and squeezed. "I know we barely know each other, but I meant what I said."

Karli tilted her head to the side. "What was it that you said?"

Cade smirked. "I love you, Karli Sloane."

"You do? I don't remember you telling me that before."

Cade shook his head. "Well, then I guess I'll have to tell you over and over again until it sinks in. I love you."

He slowly pulled her toward him until she had to sit on the edge of the bed.

"I love you, Karli."

She smiled. "You do?"

Cade nodded. "I do. Very much. It's been fast, but I've never felt like this before. When I saw you in that warehouse and knew Damon was there and planning to kill you... I would have given my life for you. I'm very grateful you saved me, though."

"You know why I saved your life?" she asked.

"Because you're a good person?"

"And because I love you, too."

"Good. Because I was going to be really disappointed if I had to let you go."

Karli shook her head. "Not happening. You're stuck with me, Cade Murray."

He smiled. "Sounds good to me."

He pulled her down for a kiss and winced the second their lips touched.

Karli pulled away as Cade reached up to his broken nose.

"Fuck, that hurts."

"I'm sorry," Karli breathed.

Cade smiled at her. "I'm not letting that sick bastard take this moment from us. I love you."

Karli smiled back. "He's not going to take anything else from us." She leaned down and carefully avoided Cade's nose with hers. She gave him a quick kiss, one that was far from the kiss she wanted to give him, but it was enough. It was a promise that their story was only just beginning.

19

———————

Cade was beyond ready to get the hell out of the hospital. They were taking excellent care of him, but he wanted to go to the bathroom without a witness and take a shower and wear his own damn clothes.

"Good news, Mr. Murray. You can go home today," the doctor said when he walked in.

"No shit," Cade replied.

The doctor chuckled. "Yes, sir. I have your discharge paperwork here for you. I have been assured you will have around the clock care until you're feeling better, so I have no reason to keep you here any longer."

Cade looked at Karli and winked. She promised she wouldn't leave his side until he was healed.

"No funny business, you two. No strenuous activities for at least six weeks. Those ribs need to heal. That means you need to do your breathing exercises, but no sex. Even if you tell me it makes you breathe hard. I've heard all the jokes before."

Cade laughed, especially when he saw Karli's eyes get huge. "I think you embarrassed her, doc."

"Then hopefully she'll listen. You'll both be a lot more embarrassed if you come back here in a few weeks with a worse injury to those ribs or pneumonia because you didn't follow my instructions."

"We will, doctor. I promise," Karli assured him.

"Good. Now, Mr. Murray, sign your paperwork, and we'll get you a ride out of here."

Cade signed everything and thanked the doctor. A nurse came in to help him change into his clothes. Marcus took Karli to his apartment the day before to get a few things. He wasn't sure how he felt about going back there now, but he didn't believe they had much of a choice.

"Braden offered to let us stay at his house while you recover," Karli said when he was dressed and they were waiting for someone to come with a wheelchair.

"Really? That's kind of a big imposition."

Karli nodded. "I said the same thing, but I think it might be for the best. Damon knows who you are. And you can't really defend yourself right now."

"I know," Cade growled. He'd been worried about the same thing since he woke up in the hospital. If Damon came after them again, he could easily get to Karli. He'd never be able to forgive himself if she got hurt because he was injured.

"The only other option is to stay with my cousin."

"Your cousin?"

Karli nodded. "She's an FBI agent. She and her partner are coming here to protect Raina. The case against Damon has become bigger. Since he admitted to knowing who Edie was, it's kidnapping, which is FBI jurisdiction. They're going to support the local agents. Her partner's cousin works with F-BOMB."

"They're all staying together?"

"No. Lorelei and Adam have a safe house where they're going to be keeping Raina. Since they're not locals, the thought is Damon and whoever else he's working with won't think of them as targets. They can operate mostly as usual."

"That's smart. Wouldn't us being there possibly mess that up, though?"

"If we stayed with them, we'd have to stay inside until we leave. We wouldn't be able to come and go."

"Which might be for the best, anyway."

Karli nodded, her gaze straying from Cade's.

"You're scared."

She nibbled her lip.

"And I can't protect you. Would you feel better going to the safe house?"

"Yes," Karli whispered.

Cade grabbed her hand and pulled her to him. The twinge in his ribs was worth it. She sank to the bed beside him as a tear rolled down her cheek. Cade wiped it away and lifted her chin with a finger underneath. "I'm sorry all of this happened to you."

She forced a smile. "It happened to us. I just hope you don't decide one day that I'm too much drama or all of this was just adrenaline and not real."

"Not a chance. This is real for me. I'm not going anywhere without you."

She smiled and leaned toward him just as someone walked in with a wheelchair.

"Okay, here we go," the man said. He smiled widely at them, his happiness infectious even though he interrupted the moment.

"Thank you," Cade said.

Karli stood and grabbed his things, slinging the bag all their stuff was in over her shoulder.

The man locked the wheels and came around to Cade's side. He held out his hand, letting Cade stand and shuffle to the seat, but there in case Cade needed the help.

He chatted as he wheeled Cade to the elevator and down to the ground floor. When a black SUV parked in front of the door, Cade tensed for a second, until Karli stepped forward and said it was Lorelei and Adam.

"Is everything okay, Mr. Murray?" the orderly asked.

"Great. Thank you for your help."

"You're so welcome. I hope you feel better soon and enjoy your day."

"You, too." Cade took the man's hand as he stood and let him help Cade into the backseat of the large SUV. Cade nodded at the man and thanked him once more before he closed the door and turned the wheelchair around and headed back inside.

"Are you okay?" Karli asked as she sat next to him in the back.

"Just getting paranoid. I thought for sure he was bringing me out to Damon or something."

Karli put her hand on Cade's knee. He wrapped his hand around hers and held on. They were safe, but they still had work to do.

KARLI WOKE the next morning and reached across the bed. The sheets were cold. She sat up and looked around, but Cade wasn't in the room.

She grabbed a sweatshirt and stuck her feet into slippers she borrowed from Jessica. After Lorelei and Adam picked them up from the hospital, they all agreed it was a good idea for Karli and Cade to stay with Braden and

Jessica for one night, then go to the safe house. They wanted to get their things together before they disappeared for a while. And they were planning a press conference.

Karli opened the bedroom door and walked down the hall. The house was still mostly dark, but there was a light on in the kitchen. That was where she found Cade.

"Hey," she said softly.

He looked up from his phone and smiled at her. He reached for her but winced with the movement.

"I hate that he did this to you," Karli said, dropping to the seat next to him.

"Better me than you. Or Raina. You saved me. He would have killed me if you hadn't come. I'll forever be grateful to you for that."

"But?"

He shook his head. "But nothing. I was just thinking I wouldn't have woken up today if Damon had his way. None of us would have. You're so brave."

Karli breathed a laugh. "I was scared out of my mind."

"You didn't show it."

She grabbed his hand and held it while she processed her thoughts. "When all of this started, I was just a regular person. Tonya walked into my apartment, and I ran. I didn't even consider confronting her or hiding or anything. I just got the hell out of there. But when Damon said you were going to die." The fear rushed back in and swamped her. Tears filled her eyes.

"You saved me."

"We all did. I couldn't have done it without Frannie and Jessica and Stacey. And having Marcus out there with the rest of the police force, I knew we would be okay."

"You amaze me. I can't wait until I can show you how

much I love seeing badass Karli standing up to that asshole."

She shivered. "I hope I never have to again, but I will if it means protecting the people I love."

Cade flipped his hand over and twined his fingers with hers. "Thank you for loving me."

Karli put her head on his shoulder, content that even though she couldn't show him her love more than that, he understood.

Jessica and Braden were up shortly after and the four of them made breakfast together. Karli laughed for the first time in what felt like forever. It was good to be with friends.

"When are you going to the safe house?" Braden asked.

"Lorelei and Adam were going to come here around noon. If that's okay."

"Yeah, of course."

"I think Frannie, Marcus, Stacey, and Wray are all going to be here then, too," Karli said, feeling guilty for having everyone invade Braden's home.

Braden chuckled. "Sounds good. Making plans for the next step?"

Karli nodded. "Yeah. We have to find Damon and make sure he doesn't hurt anyone else."

"Agreed."

After breakfast, they all took turns in the bathroom. Braden announced Wray and Stacey were bringing lunch for everyone, halting the debate Karli and Jessica were having about what they should do.

Karli sat on the couch and felt like her life was far from back to normal. She was still dead as far as the general public knew. She had no idea if she still had a job. It was the least of her concerns because she didn't want to put her patients at risk, but she missed her work.

"You doing okay?" Jessica asked as she sat next to Karli.

Karli shrugged. "I don't know. I know telling the public I'm alive is the right thing because it will bring light to Damon and force him out of the shadows, but I still don't feel like things are normal."

Jessica nodded. "I get that. When Braden works nights, I stay with Taylor and Dex. I feel like such an idiot, but I'm scared all the time."

"I didn't know that," Karli said.

"We haven't had much time to talk since you've been dead. All of this is a lot. I know Silver is dead, but knowing he was only one piece of all of this just tells me we have to find Damon and make him pay for what he's done."

"I agree. He doesn't get to steal our lives. He's taken enough from enough people. We're going to stop him for good."

"Yes, we are."

The doorbell rang out, making Karli jump. Jessica did the same, then they laughed together.

Braden opened the door to Marcus and Frannie, welcoming them in. Stacey and Wray weren't far behind them with half a dozen pizza boxes. Everyone followed them to the kitchen and started to eat while they waited for Lorelei, Adam, and Raina to arrive.

The last three weren't alone when they arrived. Dex and two other men were with them. Adam took care of introductions, telling the others one of the men was his cousin, Liam, and the other was Daniel, the leader of F-BOMB.

After everyone ate their pizza and chatted for a while, the mood in the house shifted, and Karli felt her shoulders tightening. She knew it was a conversation they had to have, but she didn't love the idea of putting herself on a stage and telling the world what happened.

"Marcus, what do you need from us?" Daniel asked as a way of starting the conversation.

"Eyes," Marcus said without hesitation. "Adam and Lorelei are leading this, but we all want the same thing. To bring Damon Street in and end the hell he's put countless people through."

"Do we have any leads on where he might be?" Dex asked.

Adam stepped forward. "At this point, no."

Everyone groaned.

"Trust me," Adam continued, "no one is more frustrated by that than we are. The plan right now is for Raina to stay with Lorelei and me at the safe house. Karli and Cade will stay with us until Cade is healed and feels safe on his own. Raina has given us a lot that's helped build a profile for Damon. He's acting in a way that indicates he's running and scared and his network is crumbling."

"Why do you say that?" Braden asked.

"He's the kind of man who's always continued with his operations as though he's untouchable. We aren't seeing that now. We're seeing him being reckless, like telling Karli to come to the place we now know was his office. He exposed his background. We know where he lived, where he worked, and we have an idea of some of his movements. In the last month or so, he's gotten careless," Adam explained.

"That should mean he's easier to find, right?" Raina asked.

"Unfortunately, it means we think he's more dangerous," Lorelei said, confirming what Karli assumed. "He's like a caged animal. He has no way out, and he's not only scared, but he has nothing to lose. When we expose him and tell everyone what he's done, he's only going to get worse."

"So, are we making the right choice?" Frannie asked.

Adam and Lorelei nodded without hesitation.

"The public has eyes everywhere. We have a better chance of finding him before he hurts someone else if we have everyone in the area looking for him," Adam said.

"Then how do we do it?" Karli asked. "How do we tell the world I'm alive, Tonya's dead, and Damon's behind it all?"

"Exactly like that," Lorelei said. "We don't sugarcoat it. We don't hide the truth. We lay it out exactly like it is and ask the public to help us bring a dangerous man to justice. His victims deserve better than to be forgotten and ignored. They deserve to have their killer rot in jail."

All eyes turned toward Raina. She hugged herself and struggled to smile at all of them. "He deserves no less."

Adam smiled at her, just a hint of a smile that he quickly schooled when he saw Karli watching him. He cleared his throat and said, "We will make sure he is brought to justice. That every person he ever hurt has their moment to show exactly who he is."

"When is the press conference?" Karli asked.

"Today at four. In front of the police station. We don't want any risk of him showing up, and he wouldn't dare with so many law enforcement officers around," Adam said.

"Are you ready?" Jessica asked Karli.

"I—" Karli stopped as a woman burst into the house.

"Stop! This is a citizen's arrest. Jessica German, you are guilty of killing... you."

Karli looked at the woman. She'd never seen her before. Her long brown hair fell in soft waves. Her pink lips were bright against her peach skin tone. The large square glasses she wore made her brown eyes look small by comparison to the frames.

"Who are you?" Braden demanded, putting himself between the woman and Jessica.

"I'm Mackenzie Chambers. I came to arrest her."

Jessica stood and moved around Braden. "I recognize your voice. You were the nine-one-one operator. You're the one who thought I killed Karli."

"You did. I know you did. But how..." Mackenzie's gaze swung to Karli and held. "You're not dead. How are you not dead?"

"I'm not, but another woman was killed in my apartment that day."

"How is this not public knowledge? The police—"

"Are aware of the situation," Marcus said, stepping forward. "I'm Captain Marcus Patrick. This is Adam Johnson with the FBI. His partner is Lorelei Sloane, sitting next to her cousin."

Adam and Marcus blocked Mackenzie from Karli's view.

"Who was the woman who died?" Mackenzie asked. Her voice pitched higher, panic setting in.

"Her name was Tonya Warren. She came here because her cousin was missing."

"Why was she killed?"

Marcus and Adam exchanged a glance. After a second, Marcus stepped forward. "Ms. Chambers, I know your story. I read your personnel file after Jessica's call. I know about your roommate."

"I didn't kill her," Mackenzie said, her voice barely louder than a whisper.

"Marcus," Karli said, standing from where she was between Cade and Lorelei. "May I?"

Marcus stepped back and let Karli through. Karli took Mackenzie's hand and led her to an open seat. Mackenzie looked like she was seconds from falling apart. Like she couldn't figure out how to piece everything together.

"I was in my apartment when Tonya broke in. I was scared, so I left through the fire escape. I didn't have my phone or ID, so when Jessica found her, and my personal items were there, the assumption was she was me. We look enough alike that it was reasonable, even I saw it when I saw her. I didn't believe it was an accident, which left me to think they thought she was me, and someone wanted me dead. The man who had her killed is Damon Street."

"Who?"

"We believe he runs a criminal organization in the area. He moves guns, people, drugs, anything he can through legal organizations that may or may not know what he's doing," Adam explained.

"Why would he care about you?" Mackenzie asked Karli.

"He didn't. He was after my roommate. She dated him without knowing who he was. She left when he almost killed her one night. He wants her back because he believes she belongs to him."

"What? No. She doesn't deserve that."

"Thank you," Raina said from the doorway. "Damon is evil. I didn't realize it until it was almost too late for me. But I'd gladly sacrifice myself if it means no one else is hurt."

"You can't do that. A man like that will never stop hurting people. I can't tell you how many calls I get every day like that. Many times it's the same woman over and over again, but they always go back. Until they can't."

Mackenzie's words sank in for everyone around. Raina hugged herself, running her hands up and down her arms. Karli reached out to her, taking her friend's hand.

"Damon thought I was dead," Karli explained to Mackenzie. "When he thought that, Raina was safer. But he knows I'm alive. And he's on the run. He also knows where Tonya's cousin is. She's alive, and we believe he can tell us where. Marcus, Adam, and Lorelei are planning a press conference for this afternoon. That's why we're all here. We're discussing what we're going to say and how we're going to get the public's help to bring Damon in."

"I promise you, I will make sure he pays. I will do whatever I can to help. I hear things. I might be able to help find Tonya's cousin. The calls I take... Let me help. Please." Mackenzie begged the room with her gaze.

"We're asking everyone to help," Adam said. "But not all of what we're going to tell you is public information. If you're willing—"

"I'm willing. Tell me what I can do. I won't stop until he's brought to justice. I promise you." Mackenzie met Karli's gaze and nodded.

"Good. Then let's get started," Adam said.

Everyone deserves justice. Even when they're no one.

Witnessing a murder was not on Frannie's bucket list.
Marcus had to find out what the curvy dancer knew.
They made a deal. She would help him, and he would find
the murderers. No one would know she was involved. She
hoped.

**Frannie and Marcus's story is available only to
subscribers.**
Sign up at https://dl.bookfunnel.com/y9ms2k2dq8 to get
FORSAKEN now.

*T*URN *the page to read chapter one of FIERCE.*

CHAPTER 1

Mackenzie Chambers shook as she hung up the phone. It was happening again. No. It couldn't. A woman was dead, and her killer was trying to get away with it.

She couldn't believe she answered both calls. After the man called, she immediately dispatched police. When he hung up, the line rang again. What were the odds Mackenzie would be the one to speak to both of them?

She knew she shouldn't have said anything to Jessica German. She should have listened and done her job. But her head spun and her heart broke and she couldn't keep her mouth shut. Not when she knew what the woman was trying to do.

Mackenzie logged off and walked away from her desk. She needed a minute. She jammed two dollars into the machine and selected a pop. It dropped to the bottom, where she grabbed it. She twisted off the top and tipped the bottle to her lips, enjoying the sweet fizziness.

"Hey, Mackenzie. How are you?"

Holden Cross. A paramedic and consummate nice guy. He was always talking to Mackenzie and asking how her day was. They ran into each other almost daily since he worked on the other side of the building. He was cute, if Mackenzie could bring herself to be attracted to him. She usually couldn't bring herself to be open to being attracted to anyone.

"Hey, Holden."

"Whoa, what's wrong?"

Mackenzie shook her head, hating that he could see through her so easily. She couldn't say the words, though. Not when she knew the look she'd get. The look she always got. She loved her job because no one judged her. Not when the only reason they called was because they needed her help. It didn't matter to them that she'd been wrongfully accused of killing her best friend.

But her coworkers were a different story. They knew her story. They knew what she'd been through. And some of them thought she was guilty.

"Rough call?" Holden asked, assessing her with his endless brown eyes. His dark hair was pushed back from his forehead in a stylish way she was surprised hadn't been messed up while he was on duty. He looked put together and perfect, counter to the disaster Mackenzie always was.

Mackenzie nodded and bit her lip.

"I'm sorry, Mack. Is there anything I can do?"

The nickname threw her. Jaclyn was the only person who'd ever called her Mack. Jack and Mack. They were a team. It had been years since she'd heard the nickname. Years since she had anyone in her life she was close to.

Mackenzie shook her head. "I'll be okay. Thanks, Holden."

"You sure?"

Mackenzie forced a smile and made a move to go around him. "I'm sure. Thanks, though."

Holden grabbed her hand and squeezed before she could get past him. His eyes were soft and kind. Understanding. It would be so easy to lean on him for a minute. Just a minute.

Mackenzie pushed away the fantasy of having someone else, anyone, to lean on. She couldn't. She had no idea who she could trust so it was better to not try.

"Thanks, Holden."

He released her, his gaze locked on her as she backed out of the room.

It would be so easy. But she couldn't give in.

Every call for the next three weeks put Mackenzie on high alert. She was determined to find Jessica German. To make sure she didn't get away with killing her friend. Mackenzie knew she was guilty. Innocent people didn't run.

She got home after another long night with no leads on where the killer was. Mackenzie was getting frustrated. Someone had to be helping Jessica German. It wasn't right.

Mackenzie turned on the news and stopped cold at the reporter's words.

"Jessica German, the woman accused of killing local art therapist, Karli Sloane, was brought into the police station last night. Another man was brought in with her, a man police are now saying was the lead suspect. Ms. German had no connection to the man, and she was released from police custody after being questioned last night. The suspect, Silver James, died before he was police were able to question him. His death is currently under investigation."

There was no way. It was not possible. Mackenzie watched the report through her tears. She couldn't believe Jessica German was going to get away with it.

Mackenzie hated that a woman died, but even more, that the woman's own friend was to blame. When she got the first call, from the neighbor, her heart stopped. But when the killer called and tried to pretend she was innocent, Mackenzie was furious.

Karli Sloane deserved better than to be forgotten. Better than having her killer go free. Jessica German deserved justice. And Mackenzie was going to make sure she got it.

Mackenzie sat in her car outside Braden Wright's house for the third night in a row. She'd watched him and Jessica German come and go for days, smiling and laughing and acting like nothing was wrong. He was living with a woman who was cold and evil. A woman who killed her friend. He could be next.

He was a firefighter, a good man. He saved people. Mackenzie couldn't sit back and let Jessica German kill him. Or anyone else. One thing she knew was people didn't stop with one. Not unless they were caught.

Mackenzie waited until the lights went out behind the drawn curtains, then sighed and accepted she wasn't going to get anything new. She drove home, hating that she hadn't been able to prove Jessica German killed Karli Sloane yet.

Mackenzie was off the next day. With any luck, she would find something. Prove something. If nothing else, she could claim it was a citizen's arrest and force the police to look into the case.

The next day, Mackenzie drove the now familiar roads back to Braden Wright's house. There were more vehicles in the driveway than usual. It looked like he was having a party in the middle of a Friday afternoon. It was the perfect time to tell them all what she knew about Jessica German.

Mackenzie snuck to the door, praying she didn't have to use the pepper spray she kept tucked in her handbag. She wrapped her hand around it just in case. Then she twisted the doorknob gently. It turned. It was unlocked.

Mackenzie didn't stop to think about what she was doing, she just acted. She burst into the house, finding the living room full of people. "Stop! This is a citizen's arrest. Jessica German, you are guilty of killing... you."

Karli Sloane sat on a couch across the room. Mackenzie knew her face, right down to the birthmark on her neck. How was she alive? What was going on?

"Who are you?" Braden Wright demanded, putting himself between Mackenzie and Jessica.

"I'm Mackenzie Chambers. I came to arrest her." Mackenzie pointed at the woman she was there for.

Jessica stood and moved around Braden. "I recognize your voice. You were the nine-one-one operator. You're the one who thought I killed Karli."

"You did. I know you did. But how..." Mackenzie's gaze shifted to Karli Sloane. "You're not dead. How are you not dead?"

"I'm not, but another woman was killed in my apartment that day." Karli's voice was even and solid.

"How is this not public knowledge? The police—"

"Are aware of the situation," another man said, stepping toward Mackenzie. "I'm Captain Marcus Patrick. This is

Adam Johnson with the FBI. His partner is Lorelei Sloane, sitting next to her cousin."

The police captain and FBI agent blocked Mackenzie's view of Karli and her cousin. Mackenzie stared back at the men. "Who was the woman who died?" Panic filled her. Something wasn't right. The whole thing wasn't right.

"Her name was Tonya Warren. She came here because her cousin was missing."

"Why was she killed?"

The police captain and FBI agent exchanged a glance. After a second, Captain Patrick stepped forward. "Ms. Chambers, I know your story. I read your personnel file after Jessica's call. I know about your roommate."

There it was. The look Mackenzie hated. The assurance that she'd been the real killer. Her argument got stuck in her throat. "I didn't kill her."

"Marcus," Karli said from behind the men. "May I?"

Karli moved past Captain Patrick and took Mackenzie's hand. Karli led Mackenzie to a seat and sat next to her.

Mackenzie swallowed her fear and emotions, both sticking in her throat as she looked at the woman she'd believed was dead.

Karli smiled kindly at her, then spoke. "I was in my apartment when Tonya broke in. I was scared, so I left through the fire escape. I didn't have my phone or ID, so when Jessica found her, and my personal items were there, the assumption was she was me. We look enough alike that it was reasonable, even I saw it when I saw her. I didn't believe it was an accident, which left me to think they thought she was me, and someone wanted me dead. The man who had her killed is Damon Street."

"Who?" Mackenzie asked.

"We believe he runs a criminal organization in the area.

He moves guns, people, drugs, anything he can through legal organizations that may or may not know what he's doing," the FBI agent explained.

"Why would he care about you?" Mackenzie asked Karli.

"He didn't. He was after my roommate. She dated him without knowing who he was. She left when he almost killed her one night. He wants her back because he believes she belongs to him."

"What? No. She doesn't deserve that." No person belonged to another. No one had a claim over another.

"Thank you," a brown-haired woman Mackenzie hadn't noticed before said. "Damon is evil. I didn't realize it until it was almost too late for me. But I'd gladly sacrifice myself if it means no one else is hurt."

"You can't do that. A man like that will never stop hurting people. I can't tell you how many calls I get every day like that. Many times it's the same woman over and over again, but they always go back. Until they can't." Mackenzie couldn't bear to think of the woman across from her going back to a man who would surely kill her. Not when he was clearly not afraid to kill people.

The woman hugged herself, running her hands up and down her arms. Karli reached out to her, taking her friend's hand.

"Damon thought I was dead," Karli explained to Mackenzie. "When he thought that, Raina was safer. But he knows I'm alive. And he's on the run. He also knows where Tonya's cousin is. She's alive, and we believe he can tell us where. Marcus, Adam, and Lorelei are planning a press conference for this afternoon. That's why we're all here. We're discussing what we're going to say and how we're going to get the public's help to bring Damon in."

"I promise you, I will make sure he pays. I will do whatever I can to help. I hear things. I might be able to help find Tonya's cousin. The calls I take... Let me help. Please." Mackenzie looked around the room at the group gathered there. She wasn't sure she was wrong about the situation, but if she was, she was not going to let a man like that go free.

"We're asking everyone to help," the FBI agent said. "But not all of what we're going to tell you is public information. If you're willing—"

"I'm willing. Tell me what I can do. I won't stop until he's brought to justice. I promise you." Mackenzie met Karli's gaze and nodded.

"Good. Then let's get started," the FBI agent said.

Mackenzie listened as they detailed what they knew so far. Damon Street was a sick man who preyed on innocent people. Mackenzie wondered how many calls she'd taken from people who were victims of his.

As they laid out their plans for the press conference, she kept her gaze on Jessica German. The woman looked ordinary. Her expressions fit what was expected when talking about a man like Damon Street, but Mackenzie wasn't convinced Jessica German was innocent. A woman was still dead, and just because it wasn't the woman they all thought, didn't mean Jessica German had nothing to do with it.

"Are you going to be able to keep all of this to yourself?" Captain Patrick asked Mackenzie.

She nodded and smiled at him. She'd never met the man before, but she knew of him. He seemed to be a man of integrity and honor. It was the only reason Mackenzie was willing to put a pin in her suspicions and let things play out.

"How is it no one knows who this man is?" Mackenzie asked. It was the question she was most curious about. If

Damon Street was so bad, how had he evaded police custody for so long?

"Damon is smart," an older woman said. "He's been working the city for decades. He knows everything there is to know about how things operate here. We believe he has a network that extends into the police department, which has allowed him to stay undetected."

"Into the police department?" Mackenzie asked.

Captain Patrick nodded. "Unfortunately, yes. We're not sure who his contact, or contacts, is, but it's unlikely he doesn't have at least one. We think that's how Silver James was killed. He was given water that had been poisoned. The officer who gave it to him has been cleared of all wrongdoing, but someone put drugs in the bottle. Someone who knew it would end up in the hands of the man who could tell us everything about Damon Street."

"Wow," Mackenzie breathed. If she didn't have trust issues before, she definitely had them after that. The police couldn't even be trusted? How would she know who to go to? What if she heard something?

"Are we all clear on the plan for today?" the FBI agent asked. He looked beyond Mackenzie to Raina, still standing in the doorway.

Raina nodded, as did everyone else.

"What plan are you talking about?" Mackenzie asked.

The others exchanged a glance. They weren't sure if they wanted to tell her the rest. She knew about the press conference, but there was more. More that she didn't know about.

"Never mind. I get it. None of you know me, and you have no way of knowing if I'm involved in this somehow. If I find out something I think could help, who should I be in touch with?" Mackenzie asked, moving on before they could make excuses for why they didn't want her to know everything.

"Me," Captain Patrick said. He stepped forward and pulled out his phone. "Put your number in here so I know it's you. I'll give you mine, too. I always have my phone with me. You can call me anytime, day or night. Please don't call anyone else on the police force. Not until we know who we can trust."

"I won't trust any of them," Mackenzie said, knowing none of them understood how true that statement was.

"We need to go," another man said, holding hands with a woman who'd been more comforting to Raina than talkative the entire time. "We have to get the boys from school."

The woman hugged the others while the man nodded to everyone.

"Thanks for your help, Wray and Stacey," Captain Patrick said. "And thanks for bringing lunch."

"The least we could do. We'll see everyone soon," Stacey said.

The others moved around, but they all seemed to be staying put. Waiting. Mackenzie realized they were waiting for her to leave.

"I guess I should go, too. Is it okay if I come to the press conference?" she asked.

Captain Patrick nodded. "Absolutely. We appreciate your help. And I'm truly sorry about Jaclyn. And everything you went through. I know it doesn't make up for it, but I've heard good things about the work you do and know it's very important. You're exceptionally kind, Mackenzie. Thank you for working with us."

Mackenzie was oddly touched by his statement. Maybe he was placating her, or maybe he was keeping her close so he could watch her, or maybe he was sincere, but his words made her trust him just a little.

Maybe Jessica German was innocent and Mackenzie had been wrong. Or maybe she was the mastermind behind Damon Street. An abusive man who'd been operating for that long didn't do it alone. He had a team. And if he was that fragile with his emotions, he usually had a boss. One who was smarter and stronger and more dangerous than him.

Was Damon the one in charge? Or did he have a boss he got his orders from? Could Jessica German be that boss?

Mackenzie was going to find out. And make sure justice was served.

Enjoy the 4th book in the steamy BBW romantic suspense series from USA TODAY Bestselling Author Mary E Thompson.

Justice is coming... because she's bringing it.

Mackenzie never wanted anyone else to go through the same hell she went through. Being wrongly accused of murder nearly broke her, but letting someone get away with murder would be worse. She was convinced she knew the truth, until she discovered the woman who was supposed to be dead was very much alive.

Holden has been in love with Mackenzie since the day they met. She's smart and stunning and completely oblivious of his feelings for her. He's finally ready to ask her out, but she has her other plans. Bringing justice to the city's most dangerous criminal. And she refuses to let Holden help.

Trust doesn't come easily for Mackenzie, but facing evil alone is not something she can do. Holden has always been kind, and she quickly learns he's also funny and smart and a damn good kisser. But none of that will help her get justice for the woman on the other end of the phone as she gasps for her last breath. A breath Mackenzie will make sure was not a waste.

READ **FIERCE** TODAY

ABOUT THE AUTHOR

USA TODAY Bestselling Author Mary E Thompson spent most of her childhood wishing she had a few less curves. She hid in the pages of books because her favorite characters never cared what size her clothes were. Now, neither does Mary, and she writes stories that celebrate women like her. Real women who have curves, chase dreams, and find love, because we should all be happy, no matter our dress size.

Mary spends her non-writing time with her husband and two kids, watching too much TV, cheering for her hometown football team (Go Bills!), and hiding chocolate from her family.

Visit https://MaryEThompson.com/ to sign up for Mary's newsletter, **Romancing the Curves**. Subscribers get free ebooks and other fun stuff, like exclusive, members only content and giveaways, plus are the first to know about new releases and sales!